honeybloods

I. S. Belle

eBook ISBN: 978-0-473-70192-5

IngramSpark Print ISBN: 978-0-473-70191-8

KDP Paperback ISBN: 979-8-871-25978-8

content warnings

You know the drill, folks! Here's where you can back out if the following doesn't sound like your cup of tea:

Gore, murder, nonconsensual blood drinking, consensual blood drinking, hints of cannibalism, underage drinking, a surprising amount of vomit, stabbing, animal death, dismemberment.

This book is to all the girls who had a weird, intense friendship with another girl that inevitably broke down in your teens, mostly (or entirely) caused by (gay) tension you didn't recognize until later.

I see you. Have some vampires.

“Sandbox love never dies.”

—— *Needy Lesnicky, Jennifer's Body*

prologue

HONEY WILLIAMS WOKE UP DEAD.

It was dark. Blood was drying in her hair. Wet leaves stuck to her bare feet. Her mouth tasted like forest and rust.

"Ugh," she croaked. "*Not* hot."

She wiped her mouth. Her hand came away red. She looked down, hoping it was water sticking the leaves to her feet.

It wasn't.

She sat up. A hand fell off her arm. It was attached to a dead cop, who lay next to her on the forest floor. *Properly* dead, eyes open and unseeing. His throat had been ripped out.

Honey ran her tongue around her mouth. A piece of flesh was wedged in between her two front teeth. Then she realized she hadn't taken a breath since she opened her eyes.

She sucked in a breath. Let it out slow. There was no relief.

"Huh," she said thoughtfully.

The night was coming back to her. She'd been at a show, the last gig before senior year started. Her boyfriend Ken had been annoying her, and there was this band whose singer kept meeting her gaze and grinning like he wanted to eat her. She wanted to annoy Ken back, so after the show she went for a ride in the band's van. For a while it was fun, no red flags in sight. They didn't even offer her beer. Then they'd pulled over at the side of the road at the edge of town. The lead singer had climbed into the back, smiling with weirdly sharp teeth.

The rest was blurry. Blood. Darkness. A cop leaning over her, then suddenly on the ground and screaming as Honey ripped his neck open with her teeth.

"Ooookay," Honey croaked. "Okay."

She shuddered, pushing herself to her feet. Her phone and wallet were missing. Her neck and wrists stung where the band members' teeth had torn into her skin. But it was almost a good hurt, like a muscle growing stronger.

A small black notebook lay on the ground next to the cop's head. Honey picked it up, flicking through the faded pages. They were filled with spiky handwriting and unfamiliar languages. She stuffed it into her bra and wiped at her bloody dress, succeeding only in smearing the blood further into the silky fabric.

"Shit." She couldn't go home like this. Her mom

would scream. Then she'd kill Honey for getting blood on the new carpet. She couldn't go to Ken's; she was pretty sure he went home with a cheerleader. She had friends, but they were party friends. Girls to laugh with in the cafeteria and go out with on weekends. Not friends who would help you bury a body.

A faint memory stirred at the back of her mind. Two girls on a swing set. A hairpin pricking their fingers. A pinkie promise: *To death and beyond, I vow to thee. Kill or die or bury a body.*

"Two roads diverged in a wood," she murmured, and set off to find the one that would lead her to Sadie Greer's house.

chapter
one

IT WAS three a.m. and Sadie Greer had puked almost all the vodka out of her system.

It had been a pretty good night. A bag of Cheetos, expertly shoplifted booze—she had a fake ID, but could rarely be bothered driving out of town to use it on a salesclerk who didn't know her—and *Gilmore Girls* reruns. This was how Sadie had spent the entire summer vacation, minus the vomiting. She could live without the vomiting.

"This is what you get for forgetting to eat dinner," she gurgled into the grimy toilet bowl. Neither she or her Dad were much for cleaning, so everything had gotten steadily grosser since Sadie's mom walked out on them three and a half years ago.

A twig snapped outside. Sadie ignored it, too busy losing another surge of bitter liquid and Cheeto chunks. She heaved twice more before her stomach quieted long enough for her to stumble up.

She wasn't always like this. Once upon a time Sadie had been an A-plus student with extracurriculars and dreams and friends—well, *one* friend. Then puberty hit and her mom left and freshman year happened. Sadie quickly discovered that even when your life was spinning out of control, you always had one thing: finding out just how bad you could make yourself feel.

"Until next time," she told the toilet. She wiped her septum piercing clean and went in search of some plain toast.

She was slotting bread into the toaster when she heard a curious noise. A low creak. Like someone was opening the front door.

Sadie froze, trying to remember if she'd locked it. No memories came back to validate this.

"Hello," she called. No answer. She picked up the butter knife from the dusty bench. "I'm—I'm armed!"

"Oooh," said a voice from the living room. "I'm terrified."

Sadie stopped. The impossibility of it took a moment to sink into her not-yet-sober brain.

"Honey?"

A rich, familiar laugh, like biting into a peach from a tree in your childhood yard. Sadie used to hear it a hundred times a day. The past few years she'd be lucky to hear it once a week, and only from a distance. Staring daggers at the back of Honey's strawberry blonde hair in homeroom, watching her make fun of someone in the cafeteria. Sadie Greer and Honey Williams were a story best forgotten. What the hell was Honey doing, walking into Sadie's house in the middle of the night?

"Are you *insane*?!" Sadie barked as she stormed toward Honey's voice.

She turned the corner into the dim living room. Honey was bending over the tattered couch, poking a finger in Sadie's Cheeto bowl and licking off the dust with a grimace. The flickering TV light illuminating her made her look like she'd been drenched.

"You're lucky my dad's not home," Sadie told her. "He would've shot you without even—"

Honey looked up. Sadie stuttered to a stop.

Honey's face was covered in blood. Her dress was stained with it, blush pink fabric turning ugly and dark as it stuck to her skin. Dirt made her golden freckles into one big smear. Her feet were bare, a leaf sticking gingerly to her ankle.

Honey grinned, teeth pink. "You *still* watch *Gilmore Girls*? Is this your whole summer vacation? Snacks, and old TV shows"—she reached into the couch cushions, unearthing the vodka that Sadie had shoved between them for safekeeping—"and booze we *all* know you're stealing from Cooper's Corner? You're lucky you tutored his kid in middle school, or he'd call the cops on you *so* fast. Get a fake ID and drive to another town to buy beer like the rest of us."

Sadie swallowed. It tasted of the liquor she'd just thrown up. "Honey. What's going on?"

Honey hesitated. "Remember when you pinkie

promised you'd help me bury a body? Is that offer still good?"

Sadie's empty stomach churned. Every second revealed another horror: muck under Honey's nails. Her dress was torn at the shoulder, exposing her black bra strap. There was, she would realize later, no bruising. No cut lip, no split eyebrow. But there was *so much blood,* blood and other things, pulp glued to Honey's tanned skin.

Honey clapped. "Sadie? Earth to Sadie? Are you fulfilling your blood vow or not?"

Blood vow. A faint memory trickled back: a swing, pinkies bleeding and hooking together. Honey kissing it better. *To death and beyond.*

Sadie unstuck her tongue from the dry roof of her mouth. "Is this a prank? Because this is...this is *so* messed up."

Honey's sunny smile faded. Her tongue moved in her cheek, an annoyed tic she still hadn't gotten rid of.

"Not a trick," she said. "It's a *very* inconvenient reality. He's out near the highway, come on."

She clapped again. Sadie flinched.

"Bury a body," Sadie repeated. Her hands tightened around the butter knife. "You want me to...did you...*kill* someone?"

Honey shrugged. She walked over to the desk drawers the TV sat on top of and pulled open the drawer with the tissues, pulling one free to wipe at her face. There was something fleshy on her chin. Like she'd gotten too excited eating a steak.

"Remains to be seen," she said, muffled in the tissue. She smacked her lips against it, as if blotting lipstick.

"Honey—"

Honey took another tissue, wedging this one in her armpit. "Look, I've had a *really* weird night. All I know is that there was this band who got me in their van and did some really messed up stuff to me—"

"Oh my god, *what*?"

"—and then I woke up in the forest with a dead guy and my mouth tastes like blood. Which, okay, actually tastes pretty good. New development."

"New *development*?" A giggle tore out of Sadie's swollen throat. "Are you telling me you're, like..." She mimed fangs. She even snarled. Vomiting only got alcohol out of your stomach, not your bloodstream. She was still pretty drunk.

Honey stood, head cocked. She had embedded a trail of grimy red footprints in Sadie's worn carpet.

Sadie blinked. Suddenly Honey was right in front of her, so close their noses brushed. Honey snarled over a mouthful of fangs, a horrifying noise ripping out her throat.

Sadie screamed and fell on her ass.

"Oh shit!" Honey laughed, bending in half with the force of it. "I didn't mean to be that intense, I swear. I just..." Her slurred speech became clearer as her teeth went back to normal.

Sadie lay there on the floor, heart pounding in her chest. "This is such a weird prank," she said, dazed.

Honey didn't respond. She was too busy placing her hands on the wall, then her bare feet. Her fingers didn't dig in, and yet she hauled herself up off the ground. Sadie watched in terrified silence as Honey scaled the wall, slow and then faster and faster, coming to a stop on the ceiling right above Sadie.

"Okay," Honey said, holding her head awkwardly to avoid bumping into the light fixture. "This is kind of baller."

She dropped. Sadie yelped, curling up like a pill bug. But Honey landed with one foot on either side of her, panther-smooth, a hand outstretched to help Sadie up.

Sadie reached up with one shaking hand.

Honey caught it and hauled her to her feet. Pain sparked in Sadie's shoulder. Honey pulled with the strength of a dog pulling a fox from a hole. When she let go, nail marks were set into the skin of Sadie's hand.

"Ow," Sadie muttered.

Honey was so close. Sadie tried to back away, but she was up against the living room wall.

Honey stepped in even closer.

"Um," Sadie said. She held the butter knife in front of her chest protectively. "What's..."

The next words died in her throat. Honey's eyes were all pupil, no ring of brown to be seen. Her pink lips parted. Her teeth were growing again, sharp points that made Sadie shudder.

Honey's gaze flickered. Tracking any movement. Her shoulders were down, her head perfectly still. A predator watching her prey. Up this close, Sadie could smell the blood. It was thick and pungent, undercut by that musty stink of forest and rot.

She smelled like death.

Not a prank, Sadie realized, stomach lurching violently.

Honey swayed forward, her soft body pressing against Sadie's sharp angles. Her black eyes fixed on the pulse point in Sadie's neck. The butter knife gleamed between them, forgotten.

"Honey," Sadie whispered. She cleared her throat. Honey watched it bob.

"Back up," she tried. "Right now. Personal space. I want it."

Honey's head twitched down toward her neck. Her lips opened against Sadie's skin, brushing the strap of her guitar pick necklace away. Her teeth formed razorblade points. Her mouth was cold as death.

Before Sadie could think to do anything—scream, kick, jab out with the butter knife she was still clenching uselessly against her chest—Honey reared back with a grunt.

"Sorry," she said. It was the most genuine she'd sounded since she came in. She wiped at her mouth again, blood transferring from her dirty hand to her freshly cleaned chin.

"God," Sadie said. "Wait here."

She staggered over to the TV and grabbed a handful of tissues. Then she marched back and started wiping Honey down. Just her face at first, fast, efficient wipes.

Honey blinked. There was blood in her fake eyelashes. Sadie hadn't thought to touch them.

"Um," Honey said. "So. You're coming?"

"Yes," Sadie said, automatic as blood from a wound.

chapter
two

HONEY ALWAYS HAD a great sense of smell. She could identify chocolate flavors with a sniff. Same with deodorant. Last week Ken tried a gross new aftershave and she had to make him go wash it off in the school bathrooms.

This was like her sense of smell did steroids. Every breath dragged in new knowledge—there was a rabbit crouching next to a tree, the tree's branches were rotting, termites burrowed deep in the bark.

She told Sadie this.

"Great," Sadie said, with the sour disposition of someone who really didn't want to be trekking drunkenly through a forest at three thirty a.m. "What the hell do termites smell like?"

Honey took another whiff. "Mildew."

"'Cause nothing *else* smells like mildew in here," Sadie muttered, and then cursed as she stumbled on a root. "Ow! If you wanted to hold the torch so bad, why don't you actually *use* it?"

Honey had forgotten. She could see for ages. She could see the dead cop all the way from Sadie's van, which was a good few minutes' walk behind them, back on the street.

"We're coming up to it," she said helpfully.

Sadie lifted the shovels higher up her shoulder. "*Finally.* I want to go to bed."

"Might be a long time coming." Honey wasn't tired at all. She wasn't entirely sure if she *could* sleep. She didn't know the rules yet. She had a fleeting wish that the band had stuck around a while longer to show her the ropes. Then she had a flash of memory: those men holding her down so each of them could take turns sinking their fangs into her neck, her elbow, her wrist. The wish died a fast death.

She lifted the torch. A beam of light hit the corpse in the face, and Sadie gagged.

"Don't you dare," Honey warned. "That's DNA evidence."

"I'm fine." Sadie covered her mouth. It was heavy with spit, but nothing else. It was probably weird Honey could smell *that.*

"Oh my god," Sadie continued, her green eyes full of horror as she took in the dead body on the forest floor. "Is that a *cop*?"

"Ummm, what happened to ACAB?" Honey wedged the torch into a tree branch so it shone helpfully toward the corpse. He looked even worse in the harsh light. Honey hoped he was a terrible person who hit his wife and didn't use his turn signal.

"Right. ACAB," agreed Sadie, with a look that suggested she didn't remember what it stood for. Disappointing for someone who posted a decent amount about social justice. Honey didn't follow her on anything, but she did check up on her every few months to try and piece together Sadie's life. She never got far— Sadie's personal posts were nearly nonexistent. She just reposted other people's stuff and sometimes added a sarcastic tag. For a few months last year, Honey thought Sadie was addicted to coke thanks to a confusing and out of context meme.

Honey reached out her hand to Sadie for a shovel. "All Cops Are Bastards."

"I *know*," Sadie said defensively.

They dug. It was surprisingly not terrible. For Honey, anyway. Her arms never ached, her shovel never slowed. Sadie started bitching thirty seconds in. By the time they were at an acceptable depth to drop a body in, she was dripping with sweat and doing stretches after every shovelful.

"Quit being a baby," Honey told her, and stood back to admire their work. "You know what? I read somewhere that if you want to bury a body, you should do it, like, vertical instead of horizontal. Because satellites pick up holes that are sus."

"That sounds fake." Sadie collapsed onto her knees,

wheezing. She held her shovel up with her trembling noodle arms. "If I dig one more time my arms are going to fall off. Let's just—shove him in. *Horizontally.*"

Honey scoffed. "I swear your arms haven't gotten any bigger since middle school."

"No? How about this?" Sadie flipped her off.

"Oooh, *savage.*" Honey giggled. It sounded strange and eerie as it echoed through the trees.

An owl hooted in the distance. Honey turned to look at it just in time for it to take off half a mile away. She could almost see the pattern of its feathers through the dark.

"Uh," Sadie said. "Are you going to help, or...?"

Honey looked back. Sadie was crouched awkwardly at the cop's feet. There was a speck of dirt on her boxy black bangs, and Honey entertained the idea of going closer and picking it out. But they hadn't talked in three years, and Honey was covered in blood, and there was a dead body between them whose throat Honey had ripped out with her teeth.

Not the time, Honey told herself. She put her hands on her hips. "Why do you get the feet? What if I don't want his gross head with blood all over it?"

Sadie made a face. "Uhhh, because I can take any end I *want*? Because I came here out of the goodness of my heart—"

"Blood vow."

"—at *three in the morning,*" Sadie continued over her, voice rising in a way that wasn't conducive to burying a body in the woods. "To help you out. And you said that blood tastes great, so if anything, you should be thanking me for taking the feet! Now get down here!"

Honey sighed and dropped to a crouch. "This is *cold*. Cold blood is *gross*."

"Excuse me for not knowing vampire rules." Sadie braced her hands under the guy's shins, visibly trying not to gag. "Okay. Um. One, two, three?"

Honey stood. It was easy. Like lifting a box of Styrofoam.

"Oh," she said as Sadie struggled under the weight of the cop's legs. "I forgot."

She took the cop from Sadie and threw him in the hole. He hit the bottom with a dull thump, face-first.

Honey tilted her head, appraising her work. Sadie joined her.

"His feet are kind of cramped," Sadie pointed out. "And his head is—"

"We should've made it taller," Honey agreed. "And worn gloves."

Sadie cursed, wiping blood and dirt on her baggy jeans.

Honey examined the guy's back for a while. There was a bulge in his back pocket that had to be his wallet. She thought about fishing it out and checking for unpaid alimony checks, evidence of a dogfighting ring, family photos with his wife and children's face scratched out, any signs he was shitty so she could feel better. ACAB was fine in practice, but it was hard not to feel guilty about violently killing a dude. Even if he *was* part of a horrifically unjust system that needed to be dismantled.

She bent down and handed Sadie a shovel, who took it with a frown.

"Must be drunker than you look," Honey said, and pointedly scooped up a shovelful of dirt. "Now we dump it back *in*."

Sadie groaned. Honey almost expected her to throw the shovel down, tell her she was done. Maybe drive off and leave Honey high and dry in the woods while she was at it. She was surprised Sadie had even agreed to *this*. Whatever Sadie had been when they were kids, she was a stone-cold bitch now.

But Sadie took the shovel. Her thin arms shook as she dug it into the pile of dirt.

Thank you. It burned behind Honey's lips.

"Faster we finish," Honey said instead, "The faster you get to collapse on that couch and let the sweet tones of Rory Gilmore lull you to sleep."

"You know I'm a Lorelai woman," Sadie panted.

"Right." Honey grinned. "MILFs forever."

"Oh my god, shut *up*." Sadie moved like she was going to smack her with the shovel, but it thumped sadly to the ground next to her own feet. Honey didn't know if that was because of Sadie's skinny arms or because they were no longer the pigtailed girls who could smack each other at a moment's notice, or wrestle each other over a bad pun.

Honey missed wrestling. You didn't get to wrestle

with your friends after middle school. She'd tried a few times and only gotten weirded-out glares in return. And on one memorable occasion, a tit punch that left her aching for days.

Sadie looked up at her impatiently. It was a moonless night and Honey could see her perfectly. Once Honey thought she had seen every single part of Sadie Greer: every secret, every hope, every embarrassing story. The dark folds she didn't show to anyone else. They'd traded blood, slept in the same bed, braided their hair together so they couldn't be apart.

Once, Honey thought they knew each other down to their marrow.

"What are you waiting for?" Sadie asked, seventeen and unknowable. "Dig."

Honey dug.

Sadie tapped out halfway through. She stood behind Honey holding the torch. Honey thought about mentioning she could see in the dark now, but decided against it.

Once the grave was full, Honey smoothed out the dirt and kicked some leaves over it.

"Solid," Sadie told her. "Can't even tell it's a grave."

They looked down at what was clearly a badly dug grave with leaves on top.

Honey clapped, scooping up the shovels. "Awesome-sauce. Can I use your shower?"

Sadie turned to her with such exhaustion Honey had to laugh.

"What? I can't walk into my house like this. If I get one scrap of forest on the carpet, let alone *blood*—"

"Ugh. Fine, just shut up." Sadie plodded away, then stopped. "Where—"

"This way." Honey led her to the van.

A pair of black, fuzzy dice hung from the rearview mirror. Honey batted at them, trying to come up with something to say that would jolt Sadie out of her stupor.

"Eyes on the road," Honey reminded her.

Sadie grunted. She slumped against the wheel with exhaustion, eyes drooping as she drove. Honey wanted to pinch her cheek. Pull her hair. Push her into the seat and breathe in her stale scent...

Honey rolled the window down and fished the book out of her bra.

Sadie glanced over. "What's that?"

"Don't know. It was next to me when I woke up." She flicked through the pages. Spiky doodles, nonsense scribbles, dead languages. A few paragraphs in English. Then, on the front page: a familiar logo of a bat clutching a knife in its talons. The band had it on the door of their van. On their drumkit. The singer had it painted on his middle fingernails. He'd shown them to Honey, who had giggled and asked to see his tooth earrings.

That was only a few hours ago. How was that possible?

Sadie glanced down at the book. "Hey. There was an indie emo band playing at Slickers tonight, the—"

"Bleeding Bastards. Yeah. *Super* indie, barely anyone knows them. And they weren't emo, they were punk rock. *Are* punk rock." Honey pressed her dirty fingers into the pages, the paper faded with age. Who did this belong to? The singer? The drummer? The bassist? The lead guitarist, with his glitter eyeliner that Honey had asked to try on?

She scrubbed her eyelids. No glitter anymore, just grime and blood.

"Right," Sadie said. She squinted into the headlights illuminating the empty road. "So...that was them?"

"That was them." Another memory was resurfacing: their tour dates. They had given her a poster. They were heading out of town tonight. Two more shows before the week was up.

"Do you wanna..." Sadie grimaced. "Call someone about getting...attacked?"

Honey snapped the book shut. "What part of ACAB don't you understand? Besides, what would I say? *I probably ate your coworker, sorry about that.*"

"Alright, god, sorry." Sadie jerked the van into her driveway and killed the engine. She climbed out, catching herself on the window as she stumbled.

Honey stayed in the van a moment longer, lost in thought. Another idea was forming.

Sadie banged on the window. "Do you wanna shower or are you going to get more shit on my car seat?"

"Coming," Honey said. She would shower, she decided. Pick out everything from under her nails. Then she would borrow Sadie's phone and look up those tour dates.

chapter
three

CRYING IN THE SHOWER WAS, Sadie considered, a pretty normal reaction to burying a body with your ex-best friend. She had thought she was fine—as fine as she could be, considering—but then she'd climbed into the shower and spotted Honey's false eyelash on the shower handle, a drop of blood still quivering on the tip.

It was either cry or get very, very drunk, and if she started drinking now, she'd just puke it all up again.

Hence: shower crying. She couldn't get the dead man's face out of her mind—his unseeing stare; his frown lines stark in the torch light; the bloody mess of his throat. He had a mustache, just like her dad. She wondered if he also combed it every morning with a brush his daughter got him for his fiftieth birthday. The dead guy's mustache was messy, but that could've been a natural consequence of getting mauled.

And it was *Honey* who did it. Honey who sunk her

teeth into his throat and tore chunks out of him. She rubbed shampoo through her lank hair and tried to picture Honey bloody and snarling, pushing the guy into the dirt. It wasn't hard. She just had to remember the unforgiving press of Honey pushing her into the wall, fangs against her neck.

Sadie shuddered. A few hours ago, her biggest problem was eating enough Cheetos to enable her stomach to accept alcohol. Now here she was, scraping grave dirt out from under her nails while Honey Williams sat in the living room watching *Gilmore Girls* and flossing a dead man's meat from the gap between her front teeth.

The TV was on pause when Sadie came out, rubbing a towel through her hair. Honey stood near the couch in Sadie's sweatpants and sleep shirt, flipping a steak knife with one hand.

"Hey," she said. "Watch this."

"No—" Sadie gagged on her protest as Honey dragged the blade down her palm. Blood spilled, black and thick and *wrong*.

"Ew! Honey!" Sadie tried to turn away.

Honey darted in front of her. "Come on, *watch*!"

Sadie grimaced, waiting. Slowly, like a zipper closing tooth by tooth, the cut sealed back up.

Honey waggled her fingers. "Awesome, right?" She did a little dance. Sadie's borrowed sweatpants strained around her hips and stomach. They were the biggest Sadie could find, but Sadie had to shop in the kids' section sometimes.

Sadie wrenched her gaze away from Honey's swiveling hips. She'd been worried Honey would hear her crying with her...super senses, or something. If she had super scent, it tracked that she would have super hearing, right? If Honey had heard anything, she was pretending like she didn't. Which wasn't like Honey. When they were friends, Honey would take any opportunity to tease the shit out of Sadie.

"That's our last steak knife," Sadie said.

Honey held it out. Sadie eyed it, waiting for Honey to move it out of reach. Her hand twitched.

Honey held it up above their heads.

"I can't deal with this right now," Sadie said. She turned toward her bedroom and what she hoped would be a slumber so deep it would erase this whole night from her memory.

Honey appeared in front of her. Sadie blinked. She'd barely seen her move, just a blur out of the corner of her eye.

"How many powers do you *have*?"

Honey shrugged and grabbed Sadie's hand. The sound of sizzling hit the air, and Honey grimaced. She held up her hand. The skin of her palm glowed with a shiny pink burn.

"Silver," she said, and grinned. "Might want to lose the rings, babe."

"Or I just won't hold your hand," Sadie spat, hoping Honey wasn't listening to her heart race over Honey calling her *babe*. She worked a ring off her middle finger —real silver, good to know the money was worth it—and slipped it in her pocket.

Honey held up Sadie's phone. On the screen was a list of tour dates. Most of them had already passed, but there were three coming up in the next two weeks.

Sadie took the phone. "What's—"

"Road trip," Honey said. "Look—Nashville, Georgia, New Orleans. Senior year doesn't start for two weeks, we can make it to all three shows if we want."

"*Why?*" Sadie held up the phone again, examining the tiny faces onscreen, all eyeliner and spiky hair and flashy guitars. "You want to go to their shows? These guys *killed* you."

"And now I'll kill them back." Honey grinned. A dimple appeared next to her mouth. Sadie used to dream of that dimple. She still did.

"I'll make them tell me how to go back to normal," Honey continued. "And then I'll kill them!"

"What? How?"

Honey tweaked Sadie's septum piercing. "We'll figure it out."

"Wait, *we?*" Sadie backed away. "This is...this is crazy. This whole night is some messed-up fever dream, I'm asleep right now in a hospital—"

Honey pinched her.

"Ow! God!" Sadie shoved her. Honey's eyes gleamed,

and for a second Sadie thought they'd fall into one of their endless wrestling matches, many of which had happened on this very carpet. There was a glittery stain next to the TV from that time they knocked a bottle of nail polish over and couldn't scrub it out. So much of their friendship happened in this room. It felt like returning to the scene of a crime.

Honey shoved her. Sadie's feet left the ground with the force of it. She slammed back into the wall, right in the spot where she'd been a few hours ago. Her head knocked against the drywall, stars bursting in her vision.

"Oh crap," Honey said as Sadie groaned. "Shit, I'm sorry, I seriously didn't mean to do that."

Sadie crumpled to the ground. More from exhaustion than anything else. She was so damn *tired*. She wanted to sleep. She wanted to drink. She wasn't much of a smoker, but she wanted a cigarette and she wanted to somehow smoke it while drinking and sleeping.

A piece of dry bread emerged in front of her. Honey had taken it out of the toaster, where Sadie left it when she investigated the suspicious noise that turned out to be a bloodstained Honey in the living room.

Sadie snatched it and took a bite, watching warily as Honey sunk to the floor next to her in a low crouch she wouldn't have been capable of yesterday. Honey smelled like Sadie's peach body wash. She'd been the one to introduce Sadie to it, years ago. Sadie would lean over in class and smell peach on Honey's hands and get a strange, electric thrill in the pit of her stomach.

"Why me?" Sadie said through a mouthful of plain bread.

Honey rested her chin on her hands. "You can drive."

"*Summer* can drive. *Britney* can drive."

"You have your own car."

"*Britney* has that stupid BMW that her dad—"

"Yeah, and how would *Britney* react if I showed up to her house and asked her on a murder road trip?" Honey laughed. It wasn't the rich, melodious noise Sadie used to covet. This was a stuttery, pale thing that Sadie rarely heard, even in weeks when Honey had slept in Sadie's small bed more than her own.

Honey was nervous, Sadie realized. She didn't want to be alone.

Honey hesitated. Rolled her tongue in her sharp mouth and brought up her hand, pinkie first.

Sadie stared at it. The last time Honey offered her a pinkie promise, Sadie had smacked her hand aside and run out of the room. *This* room. Sadie still remembered Honey's forlorn face when she snuck a glance back.

To death and beyond, I vow to thee. Kill or die or bury a body.

"I'm not dying for you." Sadie reached up and hooked their pinkies together.

"No promises, Greer," Honey said. She smiled, and for a second Sadie forgot about anything that wasn't Honey's dimple caving in her soft cheek.

chapter
four

HONEY PERCHED on the end of Sadie's sad single bed, waiting.

Honey didn't feel like sleeping—time would tell if she even could—but Sadie did, and she did *not* like Honey's idea of practicing driving while Sadie slept in the backseat.

"Just a few hours," Sadie had said, before collapsing into bed and telling Honey to get the hell out of her room.

That was seven hours ago. Honey had considered waking her up after four hours, but *Gilmore Girls* was more interesting than she remembered, and she didn't want to annoy Sadie so much she called the trip off. She was still surprised Sadie had agreed in the first place.

But there was only so long Honey could click "next episode" before curious thoughts wormed in. Which led to Honey perching on the end of Sadie's bed, deciding how harsh she wanted to go with this.

She decided on a cool, casual pinch on the arm.

Sadie grumbled and flopped over.

Honey pinched her harder.

"Ow," Sadie mumbled. She cracked one eye open. She regarded Honey with the incredulity of a deeply hungover teenager who wasn't sure if they were still in a dream. Then she took Honey in, and her face collapsed slowly into horror.

"Oh *god.*"

Honey shushed her. "Watch this."

"*No.*" Sadie rolled over, pulling her sheets over her head.

Honey tugged them off, trailing them behind her as she headed over to tug the curtains open.

Sunlight spilled over the bed. Sadie groaned, digging her face into her pillow and completely missing Honey's triumphant pose.

"Um," Honey said, still posing. "Hello? Fun new development here? See how I'm totally not on fire?"

She spun in the morning glow. It was a relief, knowing she could still have the sunlight. She hoped this vampire situation was temporary, but if it wasn't, an un-life of constant darkness wasn't very appealing. She was a sunglasses girl.

Sadie was silent. Honey spun to a stop to find her staring groggily at the borrowed shirt Honey was wearing. It was white with two tiny black words printed on the chest: **BITE ME.**

Honey laughed. "Right? I can't believe you didn't bring it up last night."

Sadie made a wet noise in the back of her throat that communicated how exhausted, wasted, and stressed she was last night. "What time is it?"

"Almost noon." Honey pulled up a backpack from next to Sadie's bed. "I packed your clothes."

Sadie swiped the backpack from her. "You what? Get out!"

"Wooow. You're *welcome*. I'll be in the living room watching Rory Makes Horrible Life Decisions: The Show. Come on, we gotta get on the road! Google Maps says—"

Sadie threw a pillow at her. Honey closed the door before it got to her, only a little surprised when the door let forth a worrying *crack*. A tiny gold hinge rolled on the hallway carpet. Honey had snapped it off.

"Oops."

Sadie's voice floated through the lopsided door. "What was that?"

"Nothing! Hurry up and get ready!" Honey turned toward the living room to watch *Gilmore Girls* and pretend she didn't hear Sadie yell after her, asking what she'd done.

Twenty minutes later, Honey climbed into the passenger's seat.

Sadie glared.

Honey scoffed at her. "Your dad's a *handyman*. That door is, like, a ten-second fix." She didn't know if that was true, but it sounded right. She pulled her legs up onto the seat, watching Sadie adjust the rearview mirror.

Honey batted the black dice dangling from it.

"Don't," Sadie warned.

Honey settled back into her seat. "What's the van's name?"

Sadie's hand froze on the key in the ignition.

Honey grinned, pressing her tongue through the gap in her front teeth. Sadie used to *hate* this, and Honey was gratified when her nose wrinkled in response. "Don't try and tell me it doesn't—"

Sadie cut her off, jaw clenching. "Steve-van."

Honey hooted, slapping her knees.

"Shut up." Sadie flushed. The blood rising in her pale cheeks was even more appealing to Honey in the daylight.

Hunger washed over Honey in an overwhelming wave. Her teeth thickened in her mouth. She turned away to hide them, forcing another laugh.

"I'm *sorry*," Sadie snapped. "Who was it that carried around that huge fact book on insects the whole year they were eleven?"

Honey dug her nails into her palms. The car rumbled to life. Her teeth slowly melted back, blunt and useless. She flipped her hair as she turned back, slapping Sadie right in the face with strawberry curls.

"Eat glass," she said sunnily.

Sadie groaned. The van—*Steve-van*—jolted down the driveway, once, twice, before smoothing out and entering the street.

If someone had asked twelve-year-old Honey what Sadie Greer's first car would be, she would have said something pale green, clean, and well maintained. This was back when Sadie was still winning spelling bees and earning money tutoring local kids.

This van was not green, clean, or well-*anything*. Old takeout wrappers were wedged in every crevice. An empty vodka bottle rolled around near Honey's feet. The white paint was chipped, the upholstery was peeling, and the engine whined worryingly when they got above fifty miles an hour.

In summary, it was exactly the kind of car seventeen-year-old Honey would've guessed she drove. The gap between middle school Sadie Greer and the tail-end-of-junior-year version who sat in the driver's seat humming along to Metallica was a chasm Honey couldn't begin to fill.

Honey twisted to look at the backseat. More takeout wrappers and a beer bottle that wasn't as empty as she would've liked, the glass lip dribbling something wet and sticky into the backpack Sadie had emptied and repacked. Next to it, the only thing placed in the backseat with any kind of care, was Sadie's guitar.

"You know what people always forget on their

murder road trips?" Honey asked. "Guitars. I bet it's gonna be so useful. Like, if you don't have a weapon, you can just—"

She mimed swinging it.

"Don't call it a murder road trip." Sadie yawned.

Honey thought very seriously about popping her finger in Sadie's mouth. She got the book out of her bra instead, flicking through the faded pages.

"Right," Sadie said. "Creepy death book. Did that belong to the band? Does it have, like, vampire stuff in it?"

"Nothing helpful." Most of the English, Honey had realized during her enforced *Gilmore Girls* time, was song lyrics. It had been disappointing when she typed them into Google and the results were a YouTube video made by a tween who had too much time to kill and access to photos of sad anime boys.

"I mean," Honey continued. She flipped to a page with fancy writing, where the ink changed from biro to fountain pen. "There's some old language stuff. I can't find anything on Google Translate. Maybe that's useful. Or maybe it's instructions on how to get into a sex club in downtown Manhattan. We just don't know."

Sadie hummed, worrying her chapped lips. They didn't used to be that chapped. Honey would've noticed. Was she biting her lips a lot nowadays? She definitely had a lot more to stress about.

Another wave of hunger. Honey fought back a shudder.

"Hey," she said. "Are you, like...coming back to school next year? People are saying you're going to drop out."

Sadie rolled her eyes. "Oh, people are saying? People are *saying*. Who the hell is gossiping about me? Don't we have anything better to talk about in this town than some former gifted kid *maybe* dropping out? Vultures."

"Nooot hearing an answer."

Sadie's thin fingers tightened on the steering wheel. "Why'd they turn you?"

Honey turned to watch the landscape blur past. They were on a highway now, a stretch between towns with nothing for miles. "I think it was an accident. I remember...scratching him. Blood in my mouth. I must've swallowed it."

"Him?"

"The singer."

Sadie didn't respond. When Honey looked over, she had a strip of plastic from the steering wheel between her fingers. It was as long as her pinkie. Sadie pinched the plastic until it cinched off, then threw it into the backseat.

Small veins stood out in Sadie's wrists. Blood thrummed through them all the way to her heart, beating in Honey's ears like Poe's heart under the floorboards, spelling danger and doom.

Or something. Honey only read the Cliffnotes.

Her hunger grew with each mile. By the time they pulled into a motel off the highway with two and a half stars on Yelp, Honey had bitten her cuticles down to the quick.

"I know," she said through gritted teeth when she caught Sadie looking while they waited in the lobby. "Not hot."

Sadie made a face that meant *I didn't say shit.* She did that a lot in class when teachers asked why she'd scoffed at something. Sadie scoffed a lot. She had it down to an art. Honey almost wanted to ask her for lessons.

Honey wrinkled her nose at the stench of cleaning fluid. Despite it, everything was coated in a thin layer of dust. The lobby had one chair, bolted to the floor. The employee behind the front desk looked fourteen and stressed as she hammered fruitlessly at the unresponsive keyboard.

Ahead of them, a man in a business suit rapped loudly on the counter. "Excuse me? Can I get some service or do you want me to sleep in here tonight?"

The employee smiled, strained, and moved a cellphone away from her face. "I'm sorry, sir. We're having some technical difficulties. We're getting it working as fast as we—"

"Fastest you can, got it." The man jerked frustratedly at his tie. "Can't you just give me the keys? Why do you need my details?"

"It's just a requirement, sir. I don't make the rules."

"Then let me talk to your boss," the man snapped. "And can we get the AC turned on? This is ridiculous."

Sweat beaded in his frown lines. He had a lot of them. He seemed like the kind of guy who got upset a lot, mostly for stupid reasons.

"I have a very important Zoom call," the man barked. "I need to get to my room and set up the Wi-Fi!"

"Of course, sir. I'm just trying to call my manager. She's not answering."

The man let out a disgusted noise. "To hell with that. Give me some keys and I'll find a room myself."

He reached over the counter. The employee reared back, looking around in a panic.

"Dude," Sadie said. "Chill out."

The man ignored her, stretching for the keys hanging on brass rings behind the desk. He went on his tiptoes, polished boots squeaking against the thin carpet.

Hunger and anger flared through Honey's gut, both emotions so huge they were indistinguishable from each other.

A growl ripped out of her throat. "*Hey*."

The man grunted. He'd almost reached one of the keys.

Honey stalked forward and grabbed him by the back of his neck, slamming him face-first into the counter.

The employee squawked. Sadie jumped back with a small, "oh my god."

Honey leaned down. "Don't be rude to customer service workers. I worked at a pizza place last summer, and trust me: we don't get paid enough to put up with your shit."

The man squirmed, making noises muffled by the wood. It was shockingly easy to hold him down, even with one arm. Honey pressed him harder into the stained wood. A vein fluttered in his shiny forehead. A bead of sweat ran over his brow.

Honey's mouth watered. Her teeth sharpened.

"Whoa," Sadie said. She grabbed Honey's elbow. "Time to let go of the asshole. Let's not...let's just *not*."

Blood rushed underneath the man's skin, so close. It would be so easy—

"Hon," Sadie said.

Hon. Honey hadn't heard that from her for years. Judging from the look on Sadie's face, she hadn't meant to let it slip.

Another tug on her elbow. Sadie looked nervous, almost scared.

The man huffed against the wood.

Honey let him go. The man stumbled away, face red and delicious, grasping his neck.

"I'll sue you," he croaked, pointing a trembling finger. "I'll—you come near me again—"

"Got it," Honey said, and turned to the employee, digging thirty bucks in cash out of her pocket. "Could we get a room for the night? Hopefully far away from this jackass?"

The employee gave her a key with the speed of someone wishing badly to be elsewhere. "Y-you can fill in your details later."

"Thankies."

They hurried down the hall, the man's renewed yells echoing behind them.

Honey slammed the door shut. "This is bullshit. It's been a *day*. Is this normal?"

"I don't *know*." Sadie stepped further into the stuffy motel room, shoulders rigid. Honey followed her gaze—only one bed. She was going to suggest that anyway, saving money and whatever, but the way Sadie was looking at it made her think Sadie would prefer wasting money.

Honey sat down on their only bed, jiggling her knees. "I...I don't want to kill anyone else," she confessed.

"Maybe you don't need to."

Honey looked up. Sadie still had that look, shoulders up, like she was bracing herself.

"You can drink from me."

chapter
five

THE BATHROOM WALLPAPER WAS YELLOW, and not by design. Mold collected thick and black around the faucets. Sadie wondered how Miss I-Can-Smell-Termites was handling this.

"How's your nose doing right now?" she asked. "Shouldn't you be dying over all these smells?"

Honey blinked. Her eyes weren't all black, but they were getting there. Only a thin ring of golden brown remained around her huge pupils.

She was standing with her back against the door. Sadie's tailbone pressed uncomfortably into the sink. But the bathroom was barely big enough for one person, let alone two. Even as far apart as they could get, they were already so close to touching.

Honey blinked again, fast, focused. "Only thing I can smell right now is you."

"What do I smell like?" Sadie swallowed, trying for a laugh. "Old beer?"

"I...don't know." Honey swayed forward, fangs protruding over her bottom lip. "Smells good."

She looked paler. The color had gone out of her cheeks. Even her freckles were less golden than when they'd gotten into the van this morning.

Sadie suppressed a shiver and offered her hand. "Okay, well. Drink up."

Honey took it. Any brown in her eyes was swallowed up by the black. Sadie expected a joke, some annoying, low-key sexy remark—but Honey just raised Sadie's wrist to her mouth and sunk her fangs in.

White-hot pain. Sadie heard herself yell, twisting away instinctively.

Honey grabbed her elbow, holding her fast. Her grip was iron, fingers unforgiving and hard in Sadie's arm.

"Ow," Sadie whimpered. "Ow, oh my god, *ow*—"

Honey's grip tightened so hard Sadie imagined her bones creaking, bruises sinking into the skin.

She batted at Honey's head. "Okay, stop now. This really, really hurts."

Honey gurgled, sucking wetly. Blood dripped down her chin, splattering onto her borrowed Converse shoes.

"Seriously," Sadie tried, cold fear creeping up her spine. "Cut it out."

Honey sucked harder.

Sadie's head flooded with dizziness. She sagged against the sink, throwing an arm back to hold herself up. "Honey—"

Honey shoved her up against the mirror, an inhuman growl scraping up her throat.

Oh my god, Sadie thought, dazed, as glass cracked behind her head. *I'm going to die from blood loss in a motel bathroom. How rock and roll.*

She reared up and kicked Honey in the stomach. It produced nothing but an annoyed mewl. Sadie groped around desperately, searching for something, anything to hit her with—but it was a shitty motel bathroom. She couldn't smack her with a roll of toilet paper.

Honey pressed harder. Glass dusted Sadie's head. She reached up, the dizziness threatening to overwhelm her, and fumbled until she had a sharp piece of glass in her hand.

"I'm *not* dying for you," she choked, and stabbed Honey in the shoulder.

Honey's mouth unlatched from her wrist. She stumbled back. Just a little, like Sadie had pushed her. Her eyes were still black.

Sadie kicked her in the knee and ran. She slammed the bathroom door just in time to see Honey's head snap toward her, and Sadie braced herself against the door with all her strength.

There was a deep screech, a terrible impact, and Sadie went flying. She landed against the bed, pieces of the flimsy door splintered around her. She rolled to her hands and knees, back aching, wrist throbbing, waiting for more pain to come.

It didn't. Sadie looked up.

Honey stood in the ruined doorway. Her eyes were golden brown, cheeks flushed, hands over her bloody mouth.

"I am," she said, muffled, "*so* sorry."

Two showers and a trip to the closest Walgreens later, Sadie grudgingly held out her arm for Honey to bandage.

"I feel like I should get a rabies shot," she said as Honey wound the bandage around her arm. "Or stitches. Or something."

"Bite wounds don't get stitches. It seals the bacteria in." Honey clipped the end of the bandage into place and beamed. "Want me to kiss it better?"

"I will hit you with my guitar," Sadie warned.

Honey flopped down on the bed, grabbing Sadie's phone from the bedside table.

"The passcode is..." Sadie trailed off as her home screen lit up. "Wait, what? Are you a mind reader, too?"

Honey laughed. "No, bitch, your pin was always 4335. The last four numbers on your library card. Nerd."

Sadie lay down next to her, careful of her injured arm, and grabbed the phone. Honey rolled her eyes but let her take it, and Sadie tried not to remember the horrible strength that pressed her into that mirror so hard it cracked.

Honey tugged at her ripped sleeve, where Sadie had stabbed her. The skin underneath was already much smaller than the blood-ringed hole. It was healing slower than the cut she'd made with the steak knife, but if it continued like that, the skin would heal in a few hours.

"Hope this backwater town has a thrift store," Honey declared as she settled against the bed frame, leaning over to see what Sadie was typing. "You know the FBI can still see you when you're in incognito mode, right?"

"Shut up." Sadie kept scrolling through results: *how to get blood from someone*. Most were unhelpful. Even if they had a medical-grade syringe, they had no idea how to use it, and Sadie didn't trust YouTube tutorials *that* much.

"We could just cut you," Honey suggested. "And then, like, drip it into a sippy cup."

They *could*. But Sadie thought of Honey's savage gaze, her unrelenting grip, and that cold fear came rushing back. She didn't want to be alone in a room with Honey while she was drinking blood, whether she drank it from a cup or straight from the tap.

"I'm not letting you drink anybody unsupervised," she said. "We'll find somebody else, and I'll be there to make sure you don't go, uh, feral. Besides, you couldn't drink from me every day anyway. They only let women donate blood every couple of months. I'd get, like, iron deficient."

"Boo," Honey said. "Cross out Sadie."

She stabbed a little cross in the air with her fingernail. It was something she did with her popular friends at school, and it made Sadie flare with loathing. Sadie had been friends with a weird, loud little girl, and then freshman year hit and Honey turned into a gorgeous queen bee who hung out with airheads and laughed at anybody who dared to care about anything.

Honey leaned in further, chin grazing Sadie's arm. "I'm still hungry, if you cared."

"Will you try to eat me in my sleep?"

"I don't know. I've been a vampire for, like, thirty hours. Still figuring out the rules." Her chin dropped, digging sharply into Sadie's shoulder.

Sadie shoved her off. Honey rolled back, snickering, strawberry blonde hair fanning out over the thin pillow.

Sadie kept her gaze on the screen as Honey climbed off the bed and started walking around the room, stepping neatly over the shards of the bathroom door. No one had come up to check what the commotion was. *Thank God for understaffing*, Honey had muttered when they came back to find the room undisturbed, no cops on their way.

Sadie searched whether you could get sued for annihilating a bathroom door in a motel. Results were inconclusive.

Honey picked at a piece of electrical tape holding up a wall lamp. "Did you know there's a wasp that eats meat? It's called the tarantula hawk. Isn't that the most badass name you've ever heard?"

Sadie couldn't help it: she laughed. "You still do those weird animal facts?"

"I mean, I don't say them out loud anymore." She

drummed on her forehead. "But I got a lot of weird stuff up here. Figured you're used to it."

"Wish I wasn't."

Honey was quiet for a while, picking over the motel room. Sadie bent over her phone, trying to ignore nails tapping on the wall, a landline being checked, a notepad rustling. Finally, there was the familiar noise of guitar strings being brushed.

"Don't," Sadie said, and looked up.

Honey had the guitar in her hands, holding it more or less like she was supposed to.

Sadie groaned. "I said—"

"Remember our band name?" Honey grinned, giving the guitar another lazy strum. "*Honeybloods.* I'd sing, you'd be on guitar. We wrote that same song over and over again, same tune, different lyrics."

She hummed the familiar warbling tune, which always cut out in the middle to allow for screaming. Screaming, they had decided, was an integral part of the song.

"We made T-shirts," Honey added.

Sadie chewed her cheek to stop the smile. The shirts had been a present from Honey's mom. For a while they wore them at every sleepover, jumping on the bed and pretending it was a stage. Every night would end with Sadie strumming so hard her fingers hurt, Honey screaming the lyrics to whatever song they'd made up that week, always to that same stupid tune. Then they'd jump off the bed and burn their knees on the carpet, arms spread to an invisible audience.

We've been Honeybloods, good NIGHT!

"Not as good as Tarantula Hawks," Sadie said.

Honey laughed, a beat too late. She was examining the peace sign sticker on the lower bout. She pinched the edge of it, like she was about to rip it off.

Sadie stiffened. Underneath the sticker was an old pair of initials: *SG + HW 5EVA*, carved with an earring that never sat straight afterward.

She opened her mouth to tell Honey to stop it. But Honey dropped her hand, leaning the guitar back against the peeling wall with surprising attentiveness.

"Thanks for coming with me," she said, voice light and careless. "I know you had to, because of the blood vow. But still."

Sadie dug a nail into her phone case. Any reply she could think of was so pathetic it made her want to hurl.

The truth was this:

Sadie Greer had a grand total of zero friends since she burned her bridges with Honey. Freshman year had been an exercise in falling—falling out, falling behind, teacher's faces falling with disappointment as she didn't turn in homework for the third week running. Her grades plummeted so hard and so fast she decided to lean into it, ditching class and ripping holes in her jeans and smudging her eyeliner.

Admittedly it had gotten a little out of hand— shoplifting vodka had never been in the plan. Nor had getting called into the guidance counselor because she smelled and he wanted to know if she had access to a washing machine. Or forgetting to brush her teeth for a week. Still, there was something satisfying in seeing how bad you could make yourself feel. Like scratching an itch and looking down to find you've torn your skin open.

Nobody wanted to be friends with this strange new version of Sadie, which suited her fine. It was easier to fall when there was no one there to catch you. Slowly, people stopped having expectations. Stopped asking her to do better. Stopped needing things from her, and let her wallow in her small little world as it narrowed and narrowed.

Then Honey had stumbled in, covered in blood, asking for help hiding a body. It was the first time anybody had needed Sadie in years.

Exhaustion hit Sadie like a tidal wave. She wanted a drink, but drinking right after losing blood probably wasn't recommended by doctors.

"I'm going to bed," she announced.

She took her socks off and climbed under the scratchy sheets. She felt the bed dip next to her. The covers didn't move.

It took embarrassingly long for it to click. Sadie rolled over to find Honey rummaging with something on the other side of the bed.

"Uh," Sadie said, "you just gonna sit there all night?"

Honey sat up, one AirPod in, brandishing Sadie's phone. It was open to YouTube.

"No," she said. "I'm gonna go through your liked videos. See what crap you have in there." She scrolled down and gasped. "Oooh, *animals greet owners after coming home from the hospital: the ultimate compilation*. I can't wait."

"I'll stake you right through the heart," Sadie told her, and pulled the covers over her head.

chapter
six

IT WASN'T a smart idea to wake up someone you almost killed the day before by putting your face directly over theirs and breathing hard until they woke up.

But it *was* very funny. Honey insisted this the entire time Sadie battered her with a pillow. She lay there for a while afterward, basking in the feeling of a good pillow fight. Sure, she hadn't hit back, and she'd felt the impact of the pillow even less than when she was...even less than before. But it was still nice to get boisterous. She barely had sleepovers with her high school friends, let alone pillow fights. She'd missed the thrill.

She licked her back molars, where a shred of Sadie's flesh was lodged, and sat up. "I'm still hungry."

Sadie leaned out of the bathroom, brushing her teeth with a finger. She'd forgotten to bring her toothbrush, and then forgot to buy one at the chemist when they were stocking up on first aid supplies.

"We'll go find somebody," she said.

Honey could smell her from here: old sweat and blood and the two chocolate bars she'd wolfed down on the way back to the motel last night, trying to get her blood sugar back up.

"I dibs the shower," Sadie continued.

Honey lifted her armpit and sniffed. "I don't think I sweat anymore. Do I need to shower, ever, unless I ate first?"

"I mean..." Sadie ducked back into the bathroom, spitting foam into the sink. She was wearing the **BITE ME** shirt today, so baggy it looked like she was swimming in it. "If you have to drink blood every day, then yeah. Gotta wash it off. Or become a less messy eater."

"Uh-huh," said Honey. She dug her tongue around her back molars until the shred of Sadie's flesh squeezed out.

Sadie made a face, pausing in the bathroom with a ratty towel in hand. "What are you *doing*?"

The string of flesh sat heavy on Honey's tongue.

"Tying a cherry stem," she said, and swallowed.

The front desk was deserted. A box sat on top, declaring all after-hours checkouts should drop their key in the slot.

Sadie dropped it in. "Okay, so: toothbrush. Toothpaste. More snacks, I can't believe we didn't stock up on the road, what was I thinking? Then we go find someone for you to..."

Honey shushed her. There was a man coming down the stairs. He wore the same wrinkled suit he'd been in last night.

He hit the bottom step and froze. His eyes widened. "I—you psychopaths have to stay ten feet away from me at all times!"

"No way did you have time to get a restraining order," Honey said. "You don't even know our *names*."

She grinned. Her teeth weren't sharp yet, but she could smell the man's sweat. He could tell, in the deep primal part of his brain, that he was prey. That he was about to be *hunted*.

Honey looked around. There were no security cameras in this shitty motel lobby.

A bead of sweat rolled down the man's bald forehead. He clutched his motel key in one hand. Not the way a scared girl would do it, protruding from her fingers, ready to claw—but the way a confused businessman would hold a key, waiting to put it in a motel box, confused why his brain was screaming at him to run away from a teenage girl who was grinning at him like he was dinner.

Honey turned. "If I don't stop, hit me with your guitar."

"I'm not going to break my *guitar* for you," Sadie started, but Honey didn't listen. She was already running.

The lobby flashed past. The man didn't even have time to scream before Honey was on him, shoving him down into the stairs and biting hard into his neck.

Blood flooded her throat. The man wailed.

Honey reached up and slammed a hand over his mouth. It took more effort than she thought. All her instincts were telling her to bite until every vein gave way. Those instincts didn't care if people heard her victim yell. They just wanted to *feed*.

A voice filtered in through the red haze. "Alright, time to stop."

Honey heard herself growl. She sucked harder. The man whimpered against her hand, his scrabbling hands getting weaker as they battered uselessly on her back.

A presence appeared behind her. Not important.

Sadie, Honey reminded herself. *Sadie's important.*

"Seriously," said Sadie behind her. "Come back. Be Honey again. Hey. *Hey*!"

Something hit her in the spine.

Come back...be Honey again. Honey unlatched her mouth from the man's neck and twisted.

Sadie stood with her backpack raised, her feet planted, ready to strike again. Her guitar and suitcase lay on the floor behind her.

Really didn't want to risk the guitar. Honey laughed wetly.

Underneath her, the man struggled. Blood pulsed from the wound in his neck.

"Hey," Sadie repeated, stern, as if berating a cat. She got on the ground—careful, eyeing Honey the whole time—and held an empty takeout cup to the stream dripping down the man's neck.

He struck out at her. Honey caught his hand before it could connect with Sadie's jaw. For half a minute, the only noise in the hotel lobby was the man's terrified grunts and the slow drip of blood filling a plastic cup.

Honey twitched. The part of her that wanted to lunge back down, to feed, to *kill,* was still there. But it was a simmer, not a boil.

The man made a noise like a plug being pulled from a bathtub drain. His eyelids fluttered.

Sadie sat back. "I'm gonna call an ambulance." She clicked a lid over the takeout cup and handed it over. "Drink it *later*. We're rationing."

Honey nodded. Blood dripped off her nose. She wiped it, then licked her hand clean as she watched Sadie pull her sleeve over her hand and reach over the front desk to grab the landline.

"Can I get a crazy straw?" she slurred.

"No," said Sadie, and dialed 911.

The open road was more fun when you were full. The cracked roads gleamed in the summer sun, a fast song spilling from the radio. They had two hours before they would arrive in Nashville, where the concert was being held: just in time to catch the concert, slip backstage, and demand some answers from those scumbags. And then kill them, if they could manage it.

Honey nestled the cup of blood against her soft stomach. The car was warm, but not blood-warm. The cup needed to be kept close if she wanted it to stay tasty.

"Oh shit," Sadie said suddenly. "What about Ken Lu?"

"What about him?" She sucked from her boring, normal straw and picked at a fleck of blood drying on her chin. She'd changed her clothes in the backseat, but they hadn't stopped at a rest stop to wash off the leftovers.

"He's your boyfriend," Sadie said. "Right? I'm not imagining you guys all over each other in the halls all year?"

"All *year*." Honey huffed. "We've barely dated four months."

"Sure, but he's been crazy about you forever."

He's been crazy about somebody *forever,* Honey thought. Ken was a good way to pass the time. He was hot and the fun kind of bitchy. But he was enamored with Queen Bee Honey Williams hanging off his arm all pretty and perfect, not Honey in sweatpants hungover on a Saturday morning, wanting nature documentaries and hash browns.

Honey missed hash browns. With her brain, if not with her stomach.

"Surprised you were in the halls enough to notice," she said. "Uh, I think we broke up."

"What? When? You were going to sing at his birthday party. You guys were gonna be *prom king and queen.*"

Honey didn't comment on the mocking tone. That stuff mattered, no matter what people like Sadie thought. *Titles* mattered. *Events* mattered. Looking back on her yearbook in twenty years to see herself beaming under a golden crown *mattered*.

She made sure her voice was its usual petty self and said, "I'm still gonna sing at his birthday, Sadie, God. You know I never miss an opportunity to have fun and look hot. Anyway I'm pretty sure he went home with a cheerleader from another school, so yeah, probably broken up. Can't exactly check my phone to see if he's texted me begging for forgiveness."

"Wait." Sadie frowned at the road. "When did this happen?"

"Two nights ago. That's why I got in the van." Honey cuddled her blood cup closer, pressing it between her boobs like she was warming a baby bird. "I'll see him when I get back. If I even want to see him. I don't know."

She had a sudden and blazing urge for Sadie to ask if she wanted to get back with him. She didn't want to examine why, but it didn't stop her from waiting with bated breath as Sadie sat still in the driver's seat, eyes glued on the empty road ahead.

Finally Sadie said, "You let your mom know you're away, right?"

"No, I'm a giant idiot who wanted to get a missing poster put up with her face on it while I'm out assaulting random strangers across the southeast." Honey tweaked Sadie's boxy bangs, easily avoiding the smack Sadie aimed at her in retaliation. "I left a voicemail. Couldn't remember her number, though. Had to check your phone. Why *do* you still have it?"

Sadie's eye twitched. "Sim card transfers contacts. I never delete them. I really should, if I still have *your mom's* number."

Honey smiled, closing her eyes against the sun. It had been nice, finding her mom's number. *HONEY'S MOM*, it had said. Right under Honey's own number. Honey had found it while she was hanging around Sadie's room, waiting for her to come out of her stupor. She'd stood there for a long time, staring down at her own name in Sadie's contacts. She'd even gone in and edited it so her name had a little vampire girl emoji on the end. Then she'd replaced it with a heart. Then she set everything back to normal and went back to packing Sadie's least awful clothes into a backpack.

Sadie's hands flexed around the steering wheel. A ring of blood dried under her thumbnail, and Honey thought about reaching over and taking it into her mouth.

She closed her eyes. "When we get to Nashville, can we get McDonalds? I want to try something."

chapter
seven

THE CONCERT STARTED in five minutes. They were not in Nashville. Sadie had missed an exit (her fault) and then another exit (Honey's fault) and then they'd run into construction and had to take a detour. Then Sadie's phone died (*also* Honey's fault for unplugging the charger last night) and they found themselves in Lock, Tennessee. While shitty and small, Lock had a McDonald's, and by that point they'd never make it to the concert venue before it emptied out.

And here they were. Standing next to the van in a McDonald's parking lot. Waiting for Honey to stop retching so they could plan their next move.

Sadie clutched her dark phone, clicking the on-off button uselessly.

Honey shuddered. Another wet splatter hit the asphalt.

Sadie sighed. "Okay, it *has* to be all flushed out now. You had *half* of it."

Honey burped in response. She turned around, black goo staining the corner of her mouth. "Can I have my cup?"

Sadie handed it over. Honey sipped, nose wrinkling. "Ugh. It's congealing."

"Poor baby." Sadie craned her neck, looking across the deserted street. "Look, that place is still open. Let's go ask about a motel."

Lockhart Books was a secondhand bookshop that specialized in hard-to-find-books, according to a sign over the door. Another sign added that they now had security cameras pointing at the tarot section.

The counter was deserted. A wall of beads led into the back room.

Sadie leaned over the counter. "Hello? Anyone there?"

No answer.

Honey inhaled. "There's someone back there. Smells like...lavender. And cigarettes. Here she comes."

A door slammed. Fast footsteps. A middle-aged woman emerged through the beads, shoving a vape pen behind her ear. Her clothes were black, her hair was dyed dark, her lipstick even darker than her clothes. The only spot of color was a red ribbon adorned with a heart clinging tight around her neck. Sadie had never met a middle-aged goth. She'd barely met any goths, period.

"Sorry," said the middle-aged goth. "The dog got the

special edition Whitmans again. Little asshole. How can I help?"

"Um," Sadie said, suddenly flustered. "My phone died. Where's the nearest motel?"

"Out on Haberdash Street."

Honey leaned on the counter, twisting a strand of hair around her pinkie. "Can you draw us a map?"

"I have the directional skills of a toddler," the goth said flatly. "But I can charge your phone. Is it an iPhone?"

"Yes! Oh my god, thank you. Just, like, five minutes." The woman took Sadie's phone, bending down to grab a charger from below the counter, muttering about how *kids these days don't know maps, don't print out motel bookings...*

"Sadie."

Sadie turned. Honey was standing near the poetry section, batting her cup against a dreamcatcher that hung from a high shelf.

"You used to have one of these." She tugged on a rainbow crystal dangling at the bottom of the dream-catcher. "Did it work?"

Sadie ignored her, stalking over and checking the goth was busy behind the counter.

"Say we made it to the concert. How are we gonna..." She dropped into a whisper. "How do we kill those guys?"

Honey stared at her. She looked...surprised. Like she'd expected Sadie to try and talk her out of it. Then she blinked and the surprise was gone, her carefree expression sliding back into place.

"I'm, like, new. That means I'm stronger, right?"

"Why would..." Sadie pinched the bridge of her nose. "How many times are we going to do this? *We. Don't. Know. The. Rules.* Even if that's true and you're a-a superstrong newborn vampire baby, that doesn't mean you can take on four old dudes."

Honey sucked at her straw, then made a face.

"It's *congealing*," Sadie reminded her. She reached into Honey's bra and yanked out the notebook.

Honey laughed. She was obviously going for a scandalized gasp, but the laugh took over easily, a loud honk that made the goth lady look up from the counter.

"Sadie *Greer*! We are in *public*!"

"Shut up." Sadie ignored her burning cheeks to look down at the small black notebook, warm from Honey's skin. She flipped it open to the pages Honey had folded over.

"These..." She frowned, flipping faster. "These are just emo lyrics."

"Pop punk," Honey corrected.

"Whatever. Where's the vampire stuff? Instructions, or guidelines, or..." She turned another page to the unfamiliar languages Honey had mentioned. They looked... very dead. And possibly in another alphabet. Whoever wrote this had very bad handwriting.

She touched the corner of a spiky letter. "Maybe it's just more lyrics."

"I don't know," Honey said. "If I was writing shit I *really* don't want people to know, I'd do it in a dead language."

The goth lady spoke up from the counter. "You kids looking into vampire lore?"

They turned. The goth leaned on the counter, picking idly at the heart that hung from the ribbon around her neck.

She waved. A scar was in the center of her palm, white with age. "Hi. Frankie. We have books on vampire shit, but it's faster asking me. What do you want to know?"

Honey gave Sadie a look that meant *how do we do this without coming across as delusional?*

"Regular vamp stuff," Honey said when Sadie couldn't come up with anything. "But, like...*realistic* stuff. Like, say vampires existed—"

"Which they don't," Sadie added, holding the notebook behind her.

Honey laughed, slapping Sadie's shoulder a little too hard. "Duh, weirdo. *Anyway*, if they *did* exist, what would the rules be?"

"Rules," Frankie repeated. Her eyes narrowed on Sadie's baggy **BITE ME** shirt. She had smudgy eyeliner, too. Sadie's heart twisted. Did *she* want to grow up and become a small-time secondhand bookshop owner in a tiny town?

"She's writing a book," Sadie croaked. "We want it to sound, um, real."

Frankie nodded. Sadie expected her to ask questions.

"So we can go full traditional," Frankie said instead. "And do the turning into wolves and mist, sleeping in coffins, can't cross running water—"

Honey cut in. "Throw a pile of seeds at its feet and it has to stop and count them."

Frankie snapped her fingers. "My *girl*. But if you want more realistic vampires, I'd have to go with they can go out in sunlight, they don't sleep, they get all pale and gross if they don't drink enough-—"

"How much is enough?" Honey asked eagerly.

Sadie sent her a warning look, but Frankie steamrollered on like it wasn't a weird question at all.

"Depends on their age. Newborns have to drink a lot. Older ones can live off...I don't know, one or two a month? Hypothetically."

"Hypothetically," Sadie and Honey said in unison.

Frankie paused. She craned her neck, trying to look at the book Sadie had clutched behind her back.

"How do you kill one?" Sadie blurted.

Frankie grinned. "Decapitation. Fire. The *Twilight* rules. Except a stake to the heart can work on a really weak one."

"Can you...like..." Honey twisted a blonde strand around her finger, leg tilting in a way Sadie found hot and deeply irritating. Like she was trying to come across as a ditz, but also she had great legs.

"Turn someone back?" Honey finished, and suddenly Sadie wasn't annoyed about her legs anymore.

Frankie's gaze lingered on their faces, then flickered down to the battered takeout cup Honey was holding. The straw was dark. A smudge of red stuck to the lid.

Could be a milkshake, Sadie comforted herself. Could be anything.

"Hypothetically," Frankie said, less excited than before. "If you kill your own sire, you go back to normal. What's that?"

She nodded at the notebook behind Sadie's back.

"Nothing," Sadie said quickly.

Honey asked, "Do you know much about dead languages?"

Sadie stepped on her foot. Or she tried. Honey was too fast, moving out of the way without even a glance in her direction. Sadie thought back to this morning, slapping Honey with a pillow, and realized Honey had allowed every single blow. Of course she had. The way she'd held Sadie still yesterday to bite into her wrist—she could have made Sadie stop anytime.

Frankie blinked. "I couldn't draw you a map good enough to get you six blocks over and you think I know dead languages?"

Honey winced. "Right. Sorry—"

"I don't actually work here," Frankie continued. "I'm covering for a friend who had to go out of town. But my friend knows a couple dead languages. The important ones, anyway. She's back in four days."

Honey turned to Sadie, eyes wide.

"We have somewhere to be before then," Sadie said,

proud of how steady her voice was. "Like, urgently. Could we grab her number?"

"Sure. Let me—"

A dog barked. Frankie cursed, pausing in the middle of grabbing her phone from her jeans pocket. "Sorry, I gotta get the dog back in before—"

The barking got louder. A Pomeranian exploded from the back rooms, running out from behind the counter and coming to a rigid stop in front of Honey, hackles up, trembling in every limb as it shrieked.

"Oh my god," said Sadie, recoiling. Sure, it was a Pomeranian. Sure, it could only leap high enough to bite her knee. But an upset dog was an upset dog, and Sadie had never seen a dog as freaked out as the fluffball in front of her, snarling up at Honey like she had devoured her whole litter.

Frankie rushed around the counter to scoop the little guy up. "Killer, what the hell? Since when do you scream at..."

She trailed off. Honey was standing very still, head cocked, eyes fixed on the dog.

Animal watching prey, Sadie thought, and shivered.

But then Honey was back, an *aw-shucks* smile spreading over her tan face. "What a cutie! You go, bud, protect your mom."

Killer growled, snapping his tiny jaws. A thin collar circled his neck, adorned with two hearts: one red, one black.

Frankie tugged on them. "Hey. Calm down. Nobody's going to get hurt."

Killer kept shaking. Frankie kissed his forehead and went back behind the counter to grab Sadie's phone, typing a number in.

"Her name's Milly Hart," she told them as she handed it back. "I'll let her know you'll be in touch."

"Thank you *so* much," Honey said. She took the notebook from Sadie's hands and slotted it back into her bra. "You're a lifesaver."

"Uh-huh," said Frankie.

Her eyes were too knowing. Sadie felt them on her back as they walked toward the bookshop door. *Did* she know? Were vampires a big open secret in America, and Sadie was just late to the party?

"Hey," Frankie called after them. "This place you need to get to. Take the highways, alright? All sorts of weird shit in these small towns. You're not going to Maine, are you?"

They stopped in the doorway. The bell perched sideways against the top of the door, half-jingled. Sadie turned to Honey, who raised her perfectly curved brows high.

Killer barked again. Frankie shushed him.

Honey turned back. "Why? What's in Maine?"

Frankie reached up with her scarred hand to touch the heart hanging around her neck. "Nothing you want to know about."

chapter
eight

"I ALWAYS THOUGHT I'd make a hot corpse," Honey announced to the nightclub mirror, slinging her arm around Sadie's shoulders.

Sadie groaned, trying to push her off. It had been a long day of driving to Georgia after staying the night in Lock, and Honey had been irritating for most of it. Honey didn't know what it was about Sadie that made her want to poke her until Sadie threatened to drive them into a tree, but it was there when they were seven and it was still here when they were seventeen.

Honey held fast, keeping Sadie pinned to her side. "No, come on! This outfit is too good to not bask in it. And you're not too bad, either."

"Gee," Sadie said flatly. "Thanks."

She squirmed. The shirt Honey had talked her into buying at a thrift shop on the way to Georgia cut off above her belly button, the most skin Honey had seen her bare in years. Sadie had been exclusively a flannel-and-baggy-jeans girl since freshman year.

Honey dug a finger into her belly button. Sadie squawked, punching her hand away.

"Don't look so *stiff*," Honey told her. "If you look that uncomfortable, people are going to notice you. We're just two anonymous hot girls having a night out on the town. We're in the crappiest club we can find, and we're luring some sleazebag away so I can have a drink."

"And then we get arrested."

"And then we flee mysteriously into the night," Honey corrected. "Never to be seen again."

Music thumped through the bathroom wall. Honey bopped her head happily to the beat, ignoring the impending headache. The night was going off without a hitch. She'd assured Sadie their shoddy fake IDs would work, but she couldn't help but be relieved when the bouncer let them past.

"Can't we just..." Sadie made a face in the mirror. "Walk around, ask a guy for a lighter, drag him into an alley?"

"Nope."

"Why?"

"Because." Honey leaned in until they were nose to nose. "This is fun. Remember *fun*?"

Sadie bit her lip. Her voice was rough from the vodka Honey had caught her sneaking on the way here. "You and me have very different ideas of fun."

She went to push past but Honey caught her again.

"Hold still," she said, and unsheathed a tube of lipstick.

Sadie rolled her eyes. "You already—"

"Yeah, and you keep biting your lip." Honey took her chin, relishing the way Sadie fell quiet and still at the pressure. She smelled like liquor, sweat, cheap deodorant. For once her eyeliner wasn't a smudgy mess around her eyes. Honey had talked her into letting her do it winged, and Sadie had sat perfectly still as Honey smoothed the eyeliner pen along her upper lid just like the very first time. They'd been in Sadie's room, perched on her tiny bed, Honey poking her tongue out in concentration. Sadie had been deathly still under her touch, eyes tracking Honey's like a moth to a bug zapper.

That was five years ago. A lifetime. And yet Honey still had that same twisty feeling in her stomach. Back then she didn't know what it was, a faint shape in the distance she couldn't make out.

She recognized it now. Hunger, plain and simple.

She swallowed the saliva pooling in her mouth and leaned back. "There! Perfect."

Sadie's red lips parted, the same color as Honey's. Her breath hit Honey's hand. She was still holding Sadie's chin steady.

Honey dropped her hand. It was that or dig her nails in. "Let's go before I start taking a bite out of *you* next."

Sadie didn't laugh like Honey wanted her to. She just blinked, lashes heavy with the mascara she'd let Honey put on her in their motel room, and followed her out into the club.

Nightclubs, Honey decided, were more fun when you didn't have super hearing. She assumed, anyway. This was her first nightclub. She'd been to a lot of house parties and a few gigs, but she was a seventeen-year-old from a small town where the most popular form of nightlife was a bowling alley that offered free nachos on Thursdays.

Music pounded through her like a battering ram. Strobe lights made her feet tingle with adrenaline, ready to run. Too many people, and too *close*. Elbows knocked into her spine, shoulders bumping. Every time Honey moved away from one there would be another.

Honey leaned in to shout in Sadie's ear. "Remind me to buy earplugs for the gig tomorrow."

"What?"

Honey shook her head, craning to see through the crowd.

Sadie stepped closer, out of the way of a flailing dancer. "Anything?"

Honey paused in the middle of another headshake.

There was a boy standing at the bar. More man than boy, but still a boy, maybe some other teenager taking advantage of their lack of carding. He was wearing a hoodie and sandals—in a *nightclub*—and he smiled like he already knew what Honey looked like naked.

"Bingo," Honey muttered.

Sadie snorted. "You're such a dork."

Honey took her wrist and led her through the crowd. The guy's smile grew, leaning back against the bar with long, loose limbs. Waiting for her to come to him.

"Hi," Honey said, smiling like a cat. "Mind if my friend and I join you?"

Sadie glared. She had assumed Honey would take care of the seduction, and Sadie would show up at the end to make sure she wouldn't murder anyone.

Joke's on you, Honey thought. She slid onto the stool next to him, making sure their knees brushed. Her dress cut off just below her butt, showing off her legs: bare with just a tiny bit of stubble. She'd tried shaving them last night, but by the time she got out of the shower the hair had grown back.

"I'm Lorelai," Honey said. She gestured to Sadie, who was standing stiffly beside her. "This is Luke."

The guy didn't even blink. Maybe Luke was a girl's name and Honey was just late to the party. It *did* sound kind of cool. Sadie would suit a name like Luke.

"Jesse," he drawled, saluting her with his can of White Claw. "I like your dress. It's hot."

"Thank you!" Honey did a little shimmy on her stool. "I like your sandals. Free your toes, right?"

"Right." His voice was slow and syrupy as molasses. Honey couldn't place the accent. He sounded like Matthew McConaughey. "So, what brings you—"

A sharp floral smell cut through the booze and sweat

as a slim arm snaked around Jesse's neck. The girl—woman? She looked almost old enough to be legally in here—beamed at them, hand toying with his shirt collar. Her mouth was shaped like a heart. Her hair was an elegant black pile on her head, held together with a pin that Honey wanted to steal.

"I'm Jessica," the girl said. "You girls having fun tonight?"

"Totally," Honey said. She nudged Sadie.

"Totally," Sadie parroted, sarcasm only slightly marred by the elbow Honey had just dug into her chest.

Honey leaned forward, flashing her cleavage. "Jesse and Jessica, huh? Did you get together just because of the name thing?"

Jesse laughed. "Oh, we're not together. We just have fun sometimes."

"Cool." Honey rested her hand on her chin, letting her. "Me and Luke have fun sometimes. Would you want to have fun with us?"

Sadie let out a choked noise behind her.

Jesse and Jessica traded a look. Surprised, but not reluctant.

"Uhhh," Jesse said. He laughed, the sound less sure than his cocky demeanor suggested. "Yeah? I mean—"

"Not you." Honey nodded at Jessica. "Just her."

She had barely a second to appreciate their expressions—Jesse abashed and awkward, Jessica pleased and shocked—before Sadie pulled Honey around to face her.

Honey let herself be pulled. "Yes? What?"

Sadie's cheeks glowed delicious red under the strobe lights. She looked incredibly young. Like she really was back in her bedroom letting Honey put makeup on her for the first time.

Honey forced back the wave of hunger that roared through her at Sadie's blush. "Hey, it's fine. This is the plan. We're not going to do anything. We're just..."

She mimed a bite.

"I know," Sadie said, rushed. "I...you're just...never mind."

She turned Honey back around, hands on her shoulders and everything. Again, Honey let herself be turned.

Jessica pursed her heart-shaped mouth. "Everything okay?"

"She might head off." Honey leaned in, tucking a stray piece of Jessica's hair back into its bun. "Want to walk her home together?"

"Alright." Jessica grinned, twisting to press a surprisingly fond kiss to Jesse's cheek. "Take care of you."

"Yeah, yeah. You too." Jesse's smile was bitter, but Honey caught a flash of reluctant fondness creeping through when Jessica tweaked his ear. He raised his White Claw in goodbye as they left.

Take care of you. It was a constant itch in Honey's mind as she pulled Jessica into an alleyway.

Jessica went easily, giggling. "I don't see it!"

"It was the cutest cat, I swear. It ran this way." Honey dragged her further into the dark, Sadie trailing behind.

Take care of you. Jessica seemed sweet, the kind of girl Honey would befriend back home and then keep at arm's distance. Not the kind of person she wanted to hurt. But her heart beat so fast where Honey was holding her wrist, her hair so shiny, her laughter so bright.

Honey was so hungry.

Jessica's giggles tapered off as Honey pressed her into the alley wall. "Where's the cat?"

"You're the cutest cat," Honey said nonsensically, nuzzling her jaw.

Jessica turned to look at Sadie, who stood frozen next to a trashcan. "Um, are you okay?"

"She's great," Honey said, nosing the pulse point in Jessica's neck. "You're great, right, Sadie?"

Sadie gave them a thumbs-up.

Jessica wrapped a hand around Honey's cheek, tugging Honey upward.

Honey let herself be tugged. Then there was a mouth on hers, blood rushing hot under her lips. Honey felt herself gasp. She'd never kissed a girl before, sure, but she'd never kissed *anyone* while she was dead. Dead and *hungry*, teeth sharpening in her mouth, grip tightening around Jessica's thin arms.

A strange feeling built up in her fangs. Some kind of...pulsing.

She seems nice, said the small part of Honey that was still Honey. *I don't want to hurt—*

Her fangs sunk into Jessica's neck.

Jessica let out a choked gasp.

Not far away, the rustle of metal. Sadie was picking up a trashcan lid, but that didn't matter right now. Nothing mattered except the blood gushing into Honey's mouth, pumping faster the deeper she bit.

Jessica let out another gasp. That strange tingle in Honey's teeth built and built, and the gasp tapered into a moan.

"Oh," said Sadie. "My god. Um."

Jessica reached up, cradling Honey's head. She entwined her fingers in Honey's curls, and all of Honey filled with a warm glow. Nothing felt this good, not hash browns while hungover, not fumbled sex in the backseat of Ken's car, not smoothing lipstick on Sadie's bottom lip with her chin in Honey's hand—

"I'm gonna hit you with the trashcan lid now," said Sadie behind her. "Just so you know."

Honey reared back just in time to catch Sadie's arm. The trashcan lid bounced to the ground and rolled to a stop near their feet.

Sadie blinked. "Hi?"

Honey wiped blood off her chin, then licked her hand. "Hi."

Jessica sagged against her, giggling. Her arms were limp around Honey's neck.

Another stab of hunger made Honey jerk forward. Sadie flinched toward the trashcan lid on the ground, but Honey swayed back.

"I'm okay," Honey said. She touched Jessica's neck, over the bite. "You okay?"

Jessica nodded. Her pupils were blown. She shook all over. Black strands escaped her bun, falling over her dazed, grinning face.

Honey wiped at the bite with her thumb. The more blood came away, the clearer she could see it: the punctures in Jessica's skin were shrinking. Another wipe, and the bite sealed over completely.

Honey stared. "Holy shit."

"What?" Sadie hovered a hand over the trashcan lid.

Honey shook her head. Bent and licked a stripe up Jessica's bloody neck.

"You're magic," she told her. "No, wait, that's me."

Jessica's head lolled against her shoulder. Honey reached into Jessica's handbag until she found a phone, pushing Jessica's thumb to open the lock screen.

"I'm going to text Jesse to come find you," she declared. "What's his name on your phone?"

Jessica slurred, "*Jesse Shitbrain Owes Me $20.*"

"Got it." Honey kissed her hairline and started texting.

chapter
nine

SADIE WANTED to write a song about blood in motel bathrooms.

"It sounds poetic," she told Honey as she cleaned blood off her face. "Like—the imagery. I don't know. Lift up?"

Honey lifted her face. They were sitting on the floor, Honey with her back against the bathtub. Sadie swiped the wad of toilet paper down her collarbone, clearing another layer of blood. A thin trail dried between Honey's breasts. Sadie ignored it, twisting to throw the wad into the toilet bowl and grab another.

"You still write songs?" Honey tilted her head obligingly so Sadie could clean her neck. "Can I hear one?"

"I'd rather break my guitar into tiny pieces and eat it."

"One guy did that with his car."

Sadie knew. She was there when Honey read about it.

Guinness Book Of World Records. Honey got one every year for her birthday. Maybe she still did.

Honey picked a wedge of skin from between her front teeth. "So! Venom. I like the venom. Wish I knew about it when we held that guy down in the motel. Would've made it way less traumatizing for him. In the moment, anyway."

Sadie nodded, concentrating on cleaning Honey's cheeks so she didn't have to look at the shred of flesh as Honey popped it in her mouth. Alleyway blood drinking —that was song material, too. She'd turn it into a metaphor, of course. She wasn't stupid. She just knew she wouldn't be able to stop thinking about Jessica's long fingers in Honey's hair, mouth open in ecstasy as Honey sucked her blood.

Honestly, this whole road trip was song material. She could turn it into an EP. She'd made a few attempts, but nothing ever inspired her enough.

I can never let Honey know she's inspiring me, Sadie told herself. She wiped a speck of blood from Honey's ear.

"Hey," Honey said. "Can I try something?"

Anxiety fizzed in Sadie's stomach like she'd dropped a whole sleeve of mentos into a coke bottle.

"Depends," she said warily.

Honey rolled her eyes and took her wrist. She pulled Sadie's sleeve down, exposing the bandage Honey had replaced this morning.

"What are you doing?"

"Magic." Honey undid the metal clip and unwound the bandage until the bite wound showed. It looked better today, especially after they remembered antiseptic was a thing and started putting that on before replacing the bandages.

Honey's thumb hovered over the place where the bite was deepest.

Sadie's arm twitched in her grip. "Hey—"

Honey shushed her, eyes closed. She pressed down her thumb.

Sadie gasped in pain. But even before the gasp ended, the pain ebbed. A strange tingling thrummed in her wrist, deep below the skin. Her flesh was knitting together from the bottom up. The skin came last, sealing up in slow, even lines.

Honey's eyes flickered open. They were golden brown. She squeezed Sadie's unmarred wrist with a goofy smile. "Ho-ly *shit*, Sadie. Look at that! Ha-ha! I'm a *god*."

Before Sadie could process Honey being so close, her smile so lovely and stupid, that gap in her teeth so familiar it made her ache—Honey wrapped her up in her arms and hauled them up.

Honey squeaked. Sadie barely registered the sound. Honey had healed her. Honey was holding her. Honey had chosen her to share these strange days with, not her bullshit friends, *her*—

Honey's grip tightened. Sadie came back to herself with the odd sensation of air under her feet.

Honey hadn't hauled them up. Not with her legs,

anyway. They were floating closer and closer to the bathroom ceiling.

"Oh my god," Sadie blurted, staring down at the bathroom sink as it got further and further away. She clung to Honey, the only thing keeping her afloat. "Oh shit! What the hell?"

Honey burst out laughing. "Your first single! *Flying in a motel bathroom,* by Sadie Greer."

"Floating," Sadie corrected shakily. "You...this isn't that impressive. This is pretty much nothing. This is that scene in *Buffy* with Willow and Tara slow dancing a little off the ground."

Honey's eyes gleamed gold. Sadie stared. A trick of the bathroom light, or just Honey's regular shine? There were times when they were kids when the light would strike Honey in a certain way and it would knock Sadie breathless.

Honey's nose brushed her cheek. "You wanna slow dance?"

Sadie's stomach twisted. A riot of butterflies, snakes, poisonous eels. Eels could live up to eighty years. Honey told her that once. She told her that and then two months later they fell out and didn't talk for years and now here they were, floating in a motel bathroom, Honey's hands solid and impossibly strong on her back.

"I want you to put me the hell down," Sadie said. It came out harsher than she intended, and Honey's face fell.

They dropped the few feet to the tiles. Sadie landed with an *oomph*, wobbling.

Honey's arm flinched forward, like she was going to steady her then thought better of it.

"Sorry," Sadie said. "Heights."

Honey smiled. It was flimsy. "Sure. Big baby."

"Shut up," Sadie said, automatic. She bit her lip, tasting lipstick.

This motel room had a TV. Honey flipped through the channels until she found a monster movie from the sixties, then sat back against the bed.

"Just one. Again. I don't even sleep," Honey had said when they checked in. "We should just get a single."

"But where would you sit and scroll through my phone?" Sadie had replied.

On the blurry TV screen, a woman screamed. She was being dragged through a window by a man in a plastic fish suit. Sadie could see the seams.

She swallowed. "She seemed nice. Jessica. I'm glad you figured out the venom for her."

Honey looked up. A wad of cash lay on the bed that she was in the middle of counting up. Savings from her summer job last year, she'd said. Sadie was surprised there was any left.

"Me too," Honey said, and went back to counting. She was down to the coins now, sorting them into piles.

Some of them were drifting toward Sadie's knee, pulled by Sadie's weight against the mattress.

The woman on the TV shrieked louder. The fish-man was dragging her into his lake, which was obviously filmed in a studio. The scenery was painted on, the sunset rays stiff and unmoving.

Sadie sucked in a breath. "So...girls?"

The sound of coins dropping against the bed stopped. Sadie didn't dare look over.

"Like," Honey said, sounding sly but also very tired, "the general existence of girls?"

"No, like...never mind." Sadie rolled over.

Honey muttered something under her breath. It sounded like *idiot*. "Girls," she said. "Yes. I haven't...*girls*, before. But yes. Boys *and* girls."

Sadie stared at the motel wall. More peeling wallpaper. "You never said."

"Does it...make things weird?"

She said it casually, almost mocking, like she was going to laugh at Sadie if she said yes. But there was a thread of vulnerability underneath, something Sadie used to dig to find, something Honey rarely offered. And here she was, holding it out.

Sadie rolled onto her back. "Hon. I just cleaned a stranger's blood off your face. I held an empty McDonald's cup to a dude's bleeding neck so you could have a snack later. I *buried a cop* with you. We're way past weird."

Honey laughed. Her smile twisted, like she was

trying not to let it get out of control. She mimed throwing a quarter at Sadie's face.

Sadie held her hands up, just in case. When a coin didn't come, she settled back against the bed. The movie played on. She could let it lie, move on, say she had to sleep.

More screams from the TV. Sadie stared up at the ceiling and thought of flying.

"Me too," she said, rushed.

Honey paused. She was on the other side of the room now, slipping her money back into her purse. "Me too what?"

"Girls," Sadie said. "Just girls, for me. No boys."

Seconds passed. Onscreen, the hero swept the woman in his arms and kissed her with that strange, smooshy kiss that always happened in old-timey movies.

Sadie waited, expecting a joke about flannel shirts or her prepubescent obsession with Kristen Stewart.

"Cool," Honey said. She hesitated.

Sadie tensed. The vodka she'd taken a hit of before the nightclub was fading, leaving her far too sober for this conversation. She itched to go and grab it from her backpack, but she didn't want Honey to see her. Not that it would matter, right? Honey would still smell it. Sadie couldn't hide anything from her, not really.

Honey asked, "Are you seriously not going back for senior year?"

Sadie sagged in relief. "Oh. Um. I don't know. My dad wants me to, but I don't really see the point."

"Can you go back? Like, your grades have been pretty dogshit."

"Screw you, I scraped past. I can go if I want. I just..." Sadie shrugged. "Hard to give a shit about school. You know?"

Honey nodded, deep in thought. Then she sat down at the edge of the bed and didn't speak for the rest of the night.

The next night, they arrived at the concert venue an hour early. It turned out Long-Legs was a bar, something neither Google Maps nor the ticket website had informed them. Thank god for their fake IDs.

The person on the door pointed the ticket scanner at Sadie's phone. "Y'all are here early. Going to eat? We have a great burger deal tonight, half price."

Honey flashed her teeth, a beat too late. "We'll rustle something up."

Sadie waited until they were out of earshot and pulled her into the bathroom in the bar hallway. "Hey, uh. Maybe we should wait?"

"What?" Honey looked at her like she was crazy. "Why? We have the ax, matches and *very* flammable hairspray in your backpack. If it doesn't work, then we just... go back to that bookshop. Call that Milly lady."

"Sure. But..." Sadie paused. "You're tired."

Honey made a face that made it clear how insulting she found the accusation. Never mind the bags under her eyes, the white pallor to her skin. It wasn't as bad as it was before the hotel guy, but she wasn't glowing like she had been last night after Jessica.

"You shouldn't have flown," Sadie tried. "Or...or healed us."

Honey shook her off. "I'm fine."

"I just think—"

"It's FINE," Honey said, half-snarl. She turned to storm out of the bathroom.

"Oh my god, just—" Sadie followed her out into the hallway, catching her wrist. "Feed on me."

Honey paused. Her cheeks shimmered under the fluorescent hallway lights. She'd bought body glitter before they got here.

She opened her mouth. Then she stopped, head swiveling to stare at the doors at the end of the hall like a fox spotting a hunter hiding in the bushes. Her head cocked. She'd heard something.

"What is it?" Sadie hissed. She turned toward the doors. "Is it—"

The doors slammed open. A gang of men spilled out, laughing and pushing each other. They looked almost, but not quite, the same as the posters: The Bleeding Bastards' drummer had spiky blue hair and rings on every finger. The bassist was tall and gangly. The lead guitarist was short and stocky with a mustache that twirled like a carnival barker. And the lead singer had that same boyish charm, hopping in his light-up sneakers and grinning like a kid as he laughed at the drummer's joke.

They looked...*younger* than the poster. Like the people down the hall were the photoshopped version, not the poster. All their imperfections were smoothed out. They looked trustworthy. Fun. Not the type of boys who would take turns biting chunks out of a teenage girl in their van.

The singer smelled her first. Sadie watched in rising horror as he froze, smile dropping off his face. His head snapped around, taking in the two girls standing half a hall away.

His mouth dropped open. For a moment Sadie hoped he would turn and run, too afraid of the consequences he'd brought on himself. But his shock wasn't scared enough. It wasn't the shock of someone about to turn tail and run. It was simply the shock of walking into a room and seeing the last person you ever expected to see.

The horror in Sadie's stomach crystalized as his mouth hooked into a savage smile.

"Shit," he said softly. "You're fast, dead girl."

HONEY SHUDDERED. She'd tried to forget that smile. The last time she saw it, it was covered in blood and hovering over her bleeding armpit.

She grabbed Sadie's arm, scrabbling for the backpack zipper.

"We are in a hallway," Sadie hissed. "Honey—we're in a *hallway*, in a *bar*, people *will* need the bathroom."

Honey ignored her, jerking the zip open and unsheathing the ax. A mini hatchet, the sign had said. Twenty-five percent off at Home Depot.

She dropped the backpack, hoisted the ax in the air and ran. The hallway blurred, her feet moving at an unnatural speed. They even picked up off the ground. Honey didn't have time to consider how cool that was before she caught sight of the singer's smile. It was widening.

He caught her by the neck, slamming her into the wall. Honey grunted. She didn't need to breathe, but his fingers dug in hard, breaking skin. Other than Sadie stabbing her, it was the most pain she'd felt since she died.

The singer stunk like rot—all of them did —and from here it was almost enough to make her vomit. Honey tried to gag. The hand on her throat stopped her.

The singer grinned. "Guess we got too messy with our food, huh? Let some of our blood slip through the cracks? Let's rectify that."

Honey wanted to say something cool. Like, *rectify is a big word for you*. But his hand was so tight.

She swung the ax instead. Before it could connect with his stupid, grinning head, the bassist flashed forward and grabbed her arm.

Honey yanked against his grip. *I'm a newborn*, she told herself. *I can take these guys.*

But the lead guitarist grabbed her other arm, and none of her yanking was making them budge, and the hope was slowly being replaced with dread.

"Honey!" Sadie yelled. She was still standing in front of the bathroom where Honey left her. Probably good, Honey reasoned. If *Honey* was screwed, Sadie was definitely, totally, one hundred percent dead in seconds.

This is so embarrassing, Honey thought. *I didn't even get one stab in.*

Sadie reached into the backpack and brought out the hairspray and lighter.

"Don't." Honey twisted toward Sadie as much as the hand on her throat would allow. "You should—"

Before she could tell Sadie to run, the lead

guitarist pulled the ax from her grip. Honey kicked him. He doubled over, but the ax stayed in his hand. Over his shoulder she saw the drummer, watching the whole thing like it was a show he'd been looking forward to.

The singer tutted, the noise distorted by the fangs filling his mouth. His eyes drowned in liquid black as he looked at Sadie holding the hairspray and lighter.

"Sure you wanna do that, kid?"

Sadie looked beseechingly at Honey.

Honey shook her head.

The hairspray and lighter dropped to Sadie's side, shaking in her hands.

The singer leaned in. The rotting scent crept up Honey's nostrils, so thick and pungent it felt like it would never leave.

"Should've stayed home, dead girl."

Honey kicked out again. Her foot connected with the singer's knee. He braced himself, but his grip didn't falter. He held out a hand, and the lead guitarist placed the ax into it.

"Wait," Honey choked. She struggled, but it was useless—they had her arms. They had her throat. They weren't reacting much to getting kicked. And now they had her goddamn ax.

She twisted once more to look at Sadie, who had come closer, like an idiot. Her green eyes were wide and wet, her face even paler than usual as she watched Honey struggle against the singer's iron grip.

Honey wanted to say something important. She couldn't think what.

The ax rose.

Honey rasped, "Sadie—"

The ax came down.

Honey screamed as white-hot pain radiated from her neck. The cut was *deep*. He'd hit her through the collarbone, missing her useless airway but slicing through muscle and maybe even hitting her sternum. Thick red seeped from the deep wound, almost black. It stunk. Where was everybody? Somebody would definitely need the bathroom, and someone had to hear her yell if she just did it loud enough—

The ax rose again. The singer grinned, his teeth flecked with black blood.

"WE'LL LEAVE YOU ALONE!"

The singer paused. Everyone turned to look at Sadie, pale and trembling and far too close. Not close enough for a human to grab—but easy for a vampire.

Tears streamed down Sadie's cheeks.

Don't cry, Honey thought, dazed. She hadn't seen Sadie cry since—

"We'll leave you alone," Sadie begged. "We're sorry! Let her go and you'll never see us again. Just let her live."

"Not alive," the drummer murmured behind them. He twisted his skull rings around his fingers, shaking with excitement.

The singer chuckled darkly. His fingers tightened once more around her throat, just above the gaping wound. "What do you say, boys? Do we let our little mistake run free?"

All three boys laughed in response.

The singer turned back to Sadie, black eyes endless. No gold in the middle, like Honey's. These eyes went in and in and *in*.

"They say no," he said gently. "Now—"

He raised the ax.

The lead guitarist jerked, hands spasming around Honey's arm. "Boss—"

The doors swung open. A woman ran in, skidding to a stop when she saw what was going on. Her eyes widened in terror. Honey could smell sweat prickle her scalp.

"Performance art," the bassist blurted. "Practicing for, uh, the stage."

The singer nodded. His fingers dug harder into Honey's neck.

Honey nodded, too, eyes bulging.

The woman nodded along with them, lip curling back as she watched more black blood gush down Honey's front and splatter into the linoleum.

"Oh," she squeaked. "Cool."

She stumbled back out the doors.

The drummer swore. "She's gonna call the cops!"

The singer shushed him. His babyish lips tightened into a thin line, eyes tracking the wall next to Honey's head.

"Shit," he spat. He leaned in until their noses brushed. "We see either of you again—it's on *sight*."

Honey nodded. Her head span.

"We promise," Sadie said.

He nodded at his boys. They dropped her. Honey slid bonelessly to the floor, barely getting her elbows out in time to stop her head from crashing into the wet ground.

Black blood pooled on the floor. Her hands were covered in it, her front stained with the viscous liquid. *Black like his eyes,* Honey thought as she stared into it. *Black like* our *eyes.*

She watched the boys' shoes leave her vision. Their strange rotting smell got further away. The scent of peach body wash replaced it, and Honey looked up to see Sadie sink to her knees in front of her.

"On *sight*," the singer yelled. He stood at the door, the last one out.

Sadie nodded frantically. "Thank you."

The door swung closed.

Sadie pulled Honey into her lap. Her hand hovered uselessly over the deep gash below Honey's neck. She was so *warm*. Honey could feel her heat radiating through her jeans. Honey tilted her head to mouth at Sadie's denim-clad knee, smearing black ichor.

"*Not* hot," she croaked.

Sadie made a noise that could have, in another life, been a laugh. "N-*not* hot. Honey, oh my god, this is so bad..."

Honey craned to look toward the doors the woman had run out of. "Think she's gonna call the cops?"

"I don't know. Should they? Should I call a hospital?"

Honey shook her head. Black spurted down her neck, pooling in her non-wrecked collarbone. "Think a hospital...would go badly. 'M dead."

"Right," Sadie said. A tear dripped down her cheek. "Honey, holy shit, what do I *do*—"

Honey didn't hear the rest. Her vision tunneled. It took all her strength to turn toward Sadie's hand, hovering over the wound. She opened her mouth against Sadie's palm, feeling the blood pump underneath.

Then everything went black.

Dark. Silence. A minute or a million years passed before flickers seeped into the corner of Honey's vision. Someone was yelling, but it was distant, and it was hard to care when Sadie was so close.

She couldn't see her, but she could smell her. Peach deodorant and sweat and something underneath it that was uniquely Sadie, sharp and comforting.

Honey twisted toward it. Warm skin under her mouth.

"Come on," said Sadie. "*Eat*, Hon."

The skin pressed harder against her lips. A hand pulled her jaw open, setting her sharpening teeth against it. It still took a surprising amount of effort to bite down.

Blood leaked into her throat. Honey bit harder, and it turned into a flow.

"There we go," Sadie said with a sniff. She sounded pained.

Honey reached for the venom, that strange tingle that had filled her teeth in the alleyway. A low hum started in the back of her mouth.

More yelling. Sadie yelled back, "It's fine, this is all under control. D-do you like the synthetic blood? Cool, huh?"

Honey gurgled a laugh. She bit down harder.

More time passed. It was hard to tell which second blurred into the next. All Honey knew was that her hair was being tugged, her cheek pinched.

"We need to get up," Sadie said into her ear. "Okay? Move those feet. Put your back into it. I don't know if you noticed, but you're, like, twice my body weight."

Rude, Honey wanted to say. But she couldn't make her mouth work.

She opened her eyes. They were still in the bar hallway. Sadie wedged an arm under her armpits and pulled. Honey wobbled to her feet and immediately fell against the wall.

"Getting there," Sadie rasped. Her wrist was bleeding. Honey twisted toward it and almost fell again.

"Focus," Sadie barked. Her mouth skimmed Honey's forehead as she held her up, straining with effort. "Gonna get us out of here, Hon. Remember that time you had a fever on sleepaway camp and your mom was on a business trip out of state so she couldn't come and pick you up for two days? I took care of you. I bitched the whole time but you know what? I insisted. Teachers offered but I told them to shove it, I was the only one who got to take care of you. Hear me?"

Honey nodded. Her head lolled. Black blood dripped down her legs, pooling in her shoes.

Someone else was talking. Honey ignored them. The room was darker now, they were out of the hallway.

"Ignore them," Sadie told her. "Just keep walking."

Honey did. Every step hurt, every second filled with confusing scents and noises, but Sadie's voice pulled her back. One step. Then the next. The noise of the bar faded, replaced by traffic and the smell of trash.

Sadie leaned her back against a wall. It smelled like brick. When did Honey figure out what brick smelled like? Or rot, or mold, or mice. Old plastic. They were in an alley, right at the back, a bag of trash spilling over next to them.

"You're okay," Sadie said. Black blood gleamed on her chin. "I know you need it, you're okay, Hon. Here."

She raised her bleeding wrist. It was, Honey realized hazily, the same wrist Honey had healed last night. It bumped Honey's slack mouth, smearing blood. Honey's tongue darted out, cleaning it from her lips.

"I know you need it," Sadie said, green eyes steely and determined through her tears. "Come on."

Call me Hon again, Honey thought, and sunk her teeth in.

eleven

THE ONLY GOOD thing about Honey being grievously injured: it was actually possible to stop her from biting.

"Okay," Sadie gasped, pushing her back. "That's enough."

Honey mewled, straining for Sadie's bleeding wrist. Even with Honey barely conscious, it was a struggle to hold her back. Especially when Sadie's own head was swimming with blood loss.

"Gimme a second," Sadie told her, readjusting the backpack straps. Her hand ached; the wounds weren't healing. "Let me think."

Honey sagged against the bricks. For a moment Sadie thought she was just behaving. Then Honey's eyes fluttered shut.

"Crap." Sadie shook her, fingers slipping on the bloody strap of Honey's dress. "Honey? Hon!"

The back door of the bar creaked open. Sadie winced,

turning to watch the bouncer emerge awkwardly into the alley. He'd tried to help them in the hallway, but he'd backed down when Sadie screamed at him not to call anybody.

Jared, he said his name was.

"I got some water," Jared called. "If that's...helpful. Is she on something?"

"No."

"Alright." The guy stood there holding a glass of water that was wet all over, like he'd filled it in such a rush he didn't care about dripping. "So...that looks pretty damn real."

He pointed at the bleeding pit carved into Honey's neck, still oozing black blood.

Sadie laughed thinly. "Sure! Black blood disease. All the teens are getting it."

"You're crying pretty hard."

"It's a powerful piece of performance art," Sadie sobbed. She scrubbed at her face, only noticing too late that it put her bloody wrist on display.

Jared pointed. "Okay, *that* looks real."

Honey moaned. Her head shifted. More black blood slipped down her neck. It was getting...*lighter*. More vibrant. Like Sadie's blood was replacing it, going in and then straight out.

Jared took a step back toward the back door. "I think I'm gonna—"

"Wait," Sadie said. "I...help me carry her?"

He paused. "Uh. Sure, yeah, let me..."

He bent down and placed the water on the ground, hurrying over. He seemed nice. Sadie hated what she was about to do.

"Grab her shoulders," she instructed.

He bent down toward her. Honey's head lolled toward him, fangs bared.

"Jesus!" He jerked back up, his gaze darting between the two of them in growing horror. "Seriously, what's—"

Sadie grabbed his hand and dragged it down. Honey grasped it, fangs latching into the meat between his thumb and forefinger.

Jared screamed. He tried to stumble back but Honey had him by the arm, her grip tight and desperate.

"Sorry," Sadie told him. "It'll be over soon."

"GET OFF!" He flailed out, grabbing Sadie by the shirt. "GET HER *OFF*!"

"Just a few more seconds," Sadie begged.

He kneed Honey in the head. She growled, hands loosening. He kneed her again and she lurched back, just enough for him to rip his arm away and start running.

Sadie threw herself in his way. "Wait!"

He shoved her. Sadie went sprawling, scraping her hands bloody when she flung them out to catch herself.

I cannot afford, she thought as the door slammed shut, pebbles embedded in her bright red palms, *to lose any more goddamn blood. Should've landed on the backpack.*

She stood. Honey stirred against the opposite wall, her eyes cracking open.

"Sadie," she slurred. "Y'r bleeding."

"Not for you," Sadie told her, and bent down to retrieve a chocolate bar from her backpack.

It was a five-minute walk to the motel. That was what Google Maps said, anyway. It took them quarter of an hour, stumbling along with their arms around each other. Streetlights made it perfectly clear what they were wet with.

"It's fake," Sadie told everybody doing double takes on their way past. "Look, it's black. We're just two wasted teenagers going home for the night. Happy early Halloween."

Honey flicked them a salute and slurred, "Stay hydrated, folks."

Thanks to the chocolate bar and the bouncer's blood, both of them made it to their motel room without collapsing in the street.

Sadie helped Honey, fully clothed, into the bathtub. Then she slid to the floor and lay there for a good ten minutes, slowly eating another chocolate bar and googling whether she could drink after donating blood.

A resounding *no*.

Sadie sighed and dropped her phone onto the grimy tiles. "How's the gaping wound?"

Honey poked at it with a wince. "Less gapey. Numb."

"Yeah?" Sadie sat up. The cut was still awful, a hard

slice down Honey's collarbone and chest. It went almost the whole way through. But there was something inside it—the flesh was slowly knitting back together, starting in the middle and working its way outwards.

Sadie swallowed bile. "Awesome."

She grabbed her phone and scrolled further through the search results until she got to a Reddit thread. *If you drink right after you lose a bunch of blood you WILL vomit and probably faint*, a Redditor advised.

Sadie dropped the phone back on the bathroom floor in defeat.

Honey hummed, singing under her breath to a familiar tune. *"Blood in motel rooms...is less fun than you think."*

Sadie mustered a weak laugh. "Are you writing the Honeybloods song?"

"Yeah. Haven't gotten further than that." Honey adjusted her lean against the wall, smudging black into the tiles. Dark ichor matted the ends of her hair. Sadie imagined washing it out with the showerhead, tilting Honey's head back so water wouldn't get in her eyes.

She looked away. "So...do we go home now?"

"I don't..." Honey laughed hopelessly, plucking at her black-streaked dress. "I can't go home like this. What am I gonna do, steal from the blood bank? I don't even know if we have one in town."

"I mean," Sadie said. "We have a hospital."

"I don't know how it *works*." Honey curled up in the

bathtub, hugging her knees. "I'm gonna stay. I'll just... wait until he's alone. Get him by surprise."

He could still kill you. Sadie kept it behind her teeth. The singer had caught Honey so easily. He'd barely flinched when she kicked him. Even if she drained somebody dry right before she walked in, she couldn't stop him. Not without help.

Honey wiped her cheeks. Black goo, tears, glitter. "You can go home. I release you from this blood vow."

She said the last part mockingly. Like she wanted Sadie to laugh again. Like this whole trip had been a big joke, *stop taking everything so seriously, Sadie.* Even after Sadie had followed her into the woods to bury a cop. Even after Sadie let Honey bite her. Even after she crossed state lines and stabbed her and stood guard so no one saw her throw up a hash brown in a parking lot. Even after she stopped those guys from killing her and dragged her back to the motel, another in a seemingly endless string of bloody motel bathrooms.

Stupid. *Stupid.* But Sadie still thought about it: driving back home, the passenger seat empty, and slotting right back into her narrow little life. Not talking to anyone. Hiding from her dad when he tried to make small talk in the kitchen. Stealing from Cooper's Corner and drinking herself to sleep, thinking back on this trip like a bad dream she wanted to fall back into.

No one had needed Sadie in such a long time. She'd made sure of it.

She sighed. "I don't think that's how blood vows work."

Honey lifted her head.

Sadie couldn't look at her. She sniffed, scratching at a stubborn tear that had escaped the corner of her eye. "We're gonna have to stop by Home Depot again. He took our ax."

"What a bitch," Honey whispered.

Sadie's hands stung. She'd cleaned grit out of the scrapes and washed off the blood, but new blood had come in since. A drop trickled down her arm. She winced, going to wipe it away.

Honey said, "If *you're* not gonna eat that..."

Sadie hesitated. Honey's eyes were their usual brown, washed out in the light from the bare bulb of the bathroom. Her teeth were dull.

"Behave," Sadie told her, and held her hands out.

Honey was too tired to come up with a quip. She just took Sadie's hands—careful of the bite mark on Sadie's wrist—and licked, tongue strangely cold. Sadie shivered.

The pain in her scraped palms started to die. Flickers of euphoria bled up her arms, into her heart. She had to press her lips tight shut so a moan didn't spill out.

Honey lifted her head. "Is it working? The venom?"

Sadie nodded wordlessly.

"Good." Honey licked another short, hungry stripe from Sadie's palm to the tip of her finger. The bite mark on her wrist tingled.

Sadie closed her eyes. For once she was glad she

wasn't drunk. The sensations would be dulled if she was drunk. Tiny rivulets of ecstasy vibrated through her palms and zinged around her body until her hands were pink with skin and nothing else, the skin whole.

Honey didn't let go. She rested her chin on the rim of the bathtub, holding Sadie's wrists close.

"Don't bite me again," Sadie warned, hazy from the venom. "Neither of us can take it."

"Not gonna," Honey said. "Just...stay."

Sadie shuffled closer. She didn't touch Honey, didn't lean their heads together or even hold her hand. She just sat against the wall of the bathtub, crashing from adrenaline and blood loss and her second near-death experience of the week, trying not to fall asleep on the tiles.

Song lyrics itched the back of her brain. Usually she had to rummage for them. These ones came straight and clear, like they'd been waiting for her to uncover them.

Washing up in another motel bathroom / scrub that stain right outta your mouth / we swore it was womb to tomb / but I think this is gonna go south...

It sounded good. Sadie thought about getting up to write it down.

Then she fell asleep.

chapter
twelve

HONEY MISSED SLEEPING.

She also missed having a heartbeat and eating things that weren't human bodily fluids, but as she slumped against the window of Sadie's car watching the highway turn into one big blur, she *really* missed sleeping. There was a point of feeling like shit where all you wanted to do was check out, and apparently Honey couldn't do *that* unless she was on the verge of death.

Re-death. Nonexistence. Whatever.

She scratched the gash on her collarbone. The chest section had almost healed, but there was still an ugly cut gaping down her neck. If she peeled it back she could see tissue and muscle. Honey found that out this morning while they were brushing their teeth, and then spent the next ten minutes convincing Sadie not to throw up.

"Quit scratching," Sadie told her. "You'll make it worse."

"It's pretty bad already," Honey said, and stuck her finger in the numb wound.

Sadie dry-retched. The car swerved.

"*Stop* it," Sadie snapped as the car straightened back out. "That's disgusting, oh my *god*."

"You love it." Honey snickered, one of the first moments of actual levity she'd felt in the last twelve hours. It was still weighed down with worry, but that was a given. She was pretty sure she was going to feel some level of dread until her sire's head was sliced from his shoulders and she and Sadie and her were safe back home.

Sadie glowered at her.

Honey started to ask, "How long until we get to Milly's?"

A flash of gray in the middle of the road.

"Raccoon," Honey blurted.

Sadie whipped back to look, stomping on the brake so hard they both flung forward.

The car skidded off the side of the road. Neither of them stopped screaming until it jerked to a stop in the grass.

For a moment they just sat there, panting. Well, *Sadie* panted. Honey stared breathlessly down at the remains of the seatbelt in her hands. She'd snapped it in two while they were skidding.

"Crap," Sadie said. "*Crap*. Do you think it's dead?"

Honey twisted to look back. The raccoon was dragging its poor furry body off the highway just in time for another car to speed by, missing it by inches. A billboard towered in the distance: WATCH YOUR SPEED, with a bloody toddler's hand hanging out of a car window. Yikes.

"Not dead," Honey said, and climbed out.

Sadie followed her onto the grass. "Did you snap my seatbelt?"

Honey shushed her, jogging up to the raccoon as it crawled pitifully off the road. Both its back legs were crushed, and some of its lower body.

"Oh my god." Sadie came to a stop, shuddering. "I'm *so* sorry."

The raccoon emitted a low, pained whine. It took another step and collapsed. Blood leaked onto the grass.

Sadie sniffed. "Can you...can you heal it?"

"I don't know if I'm strong enough," Honey admitted. She still had the gaping neck wound, after all. Healing Sadie's hands last night hadn't helped.

The raccoon screeched again, quivering. More blood leaked out, feeding the grass, which didn't even need it. The highway was clear, no cars coming over the horizon.

Honey's eyes spasmed black.

"Oh," Sadie said. "Oh. Um."

Honey knelt down. "I'm gonna."

"No—" Sadie cut herself off, turning around.

Smart move, Honey thought, and lunged.

. . .

Five minutes later, they got back in the car. Honey sucked raccoon blood off her fingers.

"How do you feel," Sadie asked.

"Not great. Not bad." Honey twisted the rearview mirror toward her neck. The gash was still there, but it looked shallower. She couldn't see muscle anymore, just tissue.

Sadie reached into the glove box and handed her a wet wipe. Honey took it silently.

"*Twilight* rules," Sadie said, and pulled into the road.

"*Twilight* rules," Honey agreed. "Maybe I'll start sparkling. So how long until we get to Lock?"

Sadie twisted, digging the phone out from behind her. It had fallen during the commotion.

"An hour." She fitted it back onto the phone mount.

Honey nodded, sitting back to let the raccoon blood work. Hopefully they wouldn't have to talk two middle-aged women into believing it was just really convincing movie makeup.

An hour and ten minutes later, Honey knocked on the front door of Milly Hart's one-story house with a little more energy and the ugliest scarf that had ever touched her body.

Fashion over function, Sadie had reminded her before throwing it across the car. Honey had been so appalled by the paisley pattern she'd forgotten to rib her for it.

Later, she promised herself as the door swung open.

Frankie blinked out at them. Same black jeans, different black shirt. Same red necklace with a heart dangling into her collarbones. The heart glimmered in the afternoon light. Honey wanted to swallow it.

Frankie nodded at the welcome mat. "Wipe your feet and come in, girls."

Honey looked down. The welcome mat said *ROLL FOR INITIATIVE*.

Frankie led them into a tiny living room. The walls were pale and ugly, but the room was filled with so much warmth Sadie barely noticed: colorful shawls tossed over the couches, knick-knacks in every corner, photographs lining almost every surface. Group photos, mostly. People on picnic blankets, in graduation gowns, or crowded around a table with D&D dice. They looked happy. It looked like a good life. Not what Sadie was expecting for their shady translator.

"You girls look like shit," Frankie said as she sat down on one of the three couches crammed into the tiny space. "Something go down since we saw you last?"

"No," Sadie said, too fast.

Honey sunk down onto the couch opposite her. "Should've seen me last night. I looked like—"

Death shriveled to nothing in her throat as she looked at the woman sitting next to Frankie.

Milly Hart was...older. It wasn't the laugh lines around her mouth, or the thick streak of silver in her long hair. It was something intrinsic about her, something bone-deep. She looked middle-aged, but part of her was older than her bones. A woven friendship bracelet was on her wrist, obstructing a tattoo of a spiky green fruit. A scar, long and ropey, trailed across her cheek and brow. One of her eyes was gray. The other was fully white, the pupil barely visible. She looked like a kindly spirit that led you into the underworld.

"Hello," said Milly quietly. She smiled. It was stiff, but all of her was stiff. It looked like a full-time occupation, like she'd never not been holding herself like she was seconds away from bolting. "It's good to meet you. You have something for me to translate?"

"Um, yeah." Honey dug the notebook out of her bra and handed it over.

Milly's fingers twitched. The book was lukewarm with Honey's scant body heat.

Sadie gave Honey a look. *Stop keeping the evil notebook in your bra.*

Honey ignored her, watching Milly flip through the pages, touching the corners Honey had folded over. Her gaze was focused, like this was a real-life problem and not some weird theory stuff some teenage girls brought up for a story they were writing. Frankie hadn't even brought up the fake book Honey was writing. Did she know they were lying? Did they know about vampires? Was any of this helpful, or were they wasting their time when they could be looking for people who actually knew what they were talking about?

"Okay," Honey started, and the tone of her voice— no sweetness, no bullshit—made everybody look up.

"Do you actually know about any of this shit or are you just...kooky old ladies who like crystals? Because we need *help*. Not, like, vampire lore. We need actual, real-life vampire shit, because I nearly died yesterday and maybe I wouldn't have if I knew about—I don't know, *weaknesses*. Or that I'm not actually stronger because I'm a newborn, they were *way* stronger, and by the way, I can eat animals! I didn't know that! Apparently we're going off of *Twilight* rules, because it was like eating half a McFlurry when your body is screaming at you to eat, like, a steak and salad, because I still feel like shit and this still hasn't healed up!"

She yanked her scarf off. It fell to her lap in an ugly paisley heap.

Sadie made a noise that sounded a lot like *come on*. The women were silent, staring at the cut in Honey's neck. It was crusted with black. You could still see inside it: flesh, sliced veins, more black.

Frankie spoke up first. "One, I'm not even *forty*, you little shit. Two, we've had some run-ins with vamps, yeah. And trust me when I say we've seen a whole lot of other shit."

Other shit, Sadie mouthed. Honey was right there with her. What other weird magics did the world hold? Zombies? Werewolves? Were mermaids a thing? She hoped mermaids were a thing. From the way this was going they'd probably be scary mermaids with fangs and murderous intent, but still.

Honey asked, "In Maine?"

"I wish. No, this shit follows you. It's in every dark corner of this goddamn country."

"Goddamn *world*," Milly corrected softly. She straightened a corner Honey had folded over. "This is Old Dumin. It...I can't tell if it's useful."

Honey groaned. "If you say it's song lyrics—"

Milly's frown smoothed out. "There's an entry here that roughly translates to...*I hate that I don't get to hold your rough hand unless we're*...drunk? High?"

"Wasted," Sadie muttered thoughtfully. Ever the lyricist.

Honey groaned louder, throwing her head back in defeat. "I *hate* these guys. I *hate* them! I can't believe I nearly got killed *again* by some jackasses who write emo songs in their stupid little pentagram journal. Ugh."

"Okay, wait. Who almost killed you? How long has"—Frankie mimed fangs—"been going on? Who the hell are you girls? Are you both vampires?"

"No," said Sadie and Honey in one.

Frankie nodded. She was still staring at the wound in Honey's neck, nose wrinkled in disgust. Then her gaze flickered between Sadie and Honey, and the disgust faded. A small smile settled over her dark lips.

"You must be very good friends," she said.

The silence was short but damning.

"Not really," Sadie said, strained. "We just did a blood vow when we were kids."

Honey nodded, suddenly hyper-aware of how close they were sitting. Sadie's ripped jeans skimmed Honey's bare knee, then flinched back. Honey tried not to be hurt when Sadie inched away across the couch.

Same old Sadie, she told herself. *You should really be over it by now.*

Frankie nodded. "Sandbox love never dies."

It pinged in the box in Honey's head where she stored movie references. Something she used to watch a lot when she was younger.

Sadie cleared her throat. "So, how do we kill the sire? That turns her back, right?"

"Right," said Milly.

Frankie pointed at Honey. "And it *has* to be her who kills the sire."

"Cool. Got it." Sadie rubbed her hands on her jeans. They were sweaty. Honey could smell it. She'd licked those hands last night, smearing spit and venom until they healed. Then Sadie had fallen asleep on the bathroom floor, wrists limp in Honey's hands, head lolling onto the lip of the bathtub. Honey had thought about waking her up. Thought about readjusting her head so it was lying on Honey's shoulder. She'd thought about a lot of things and she ended up sitting there for hours just... staring. Watching Sadie's rise and fall. Waiting for her own cleaved-open chest to heal.

Sadie started, "So—"

Honey talked over her. "So how do we do it? Hit me with vamp weaknesses. Don't tell me: garlic? Wait, if we smash him with a van *really* fast—"

"We're not dragging my van into this."

"But—"

The front door opened and closed. Honey turned toward it. Whoever it was, they smelled like the same kind of lavender as Frankie. Lavender and clay and some spice she couldn't make out.

A woman appeared in the living room doorway. She had a cute blonde pixie cut and old, pitted scars on her arm. A black lace choker around her neck was adorned with a shiny dark heart.

"Hi," the woman said, brow wrinkling at the two teens on the couch. "Is this them? Please don't tell me we have more teenagers to babysit."

"No babysitting, Ivy, don't worry." Frankie shifted over on the couch.

Ivy sunk into place beside her. They leaned in at the same time, lips meeting in a kiss so well-worn and fond Honey's still heart twisted in her chest.

Ivy settled back against the couch, her wife's arm around her shoulder. "So," she said. "You kids have a vampire problem?"

chapter
thirteen

IT WAS strange how fast things could change.

This time last week, Sadie had been day drunk. She hadn't showered in so long her bob had started to stick to her cheeks. She'd done her usual morning trip to shove her empties into the neighbor's recycling so her dad wouldn't notice them. Then she'd collapsed on the couch and watched infomercials until she was almost talked into buying miracle skin cream with secret ingredients from Brazil. She hadn't spoken to anyone in days. She hadn't thought about Honey in weeks, if not months— not counting the flashes of irritation and betrayal she ignored whenever she saw Honey in the last few weeks of school.

Now here she was. Sitting in a stranger's living room listening to Honey explain how she got turned, dragged her ex-best friend into a murder road trip, then almost got killed (again).

As soon as Honey finished, the women turned to look at Milly.

"You've fought more vampires than us," Frankie said when Milly looked back questioningly. "And you have more experience with..."

She waved a scarred hand in the air vaguely.

"Unfortunately," Milly agreed. She scratched the spiky green tattoo on her arm, nails scraping the friendship bracelet. It looked old. There was a tiny skull woven into it that filled Sadie with curiosity and dread. A lot of the people in her photos shared that same friendship bracelet, that tiny skull glinting from everyone's wrists.

"The one time I physically fought a vampire, we had more numbers. If you're a newborn *and* they have double the people..." Milly trailed off, eyes lighting up at the guitar pick strung around Sadie's neck. "You could try Blessed Instrument."

Frankie scowled. "Don't say it like it's a D&D spell."

"Sorry." Milly gestured at Sadie's necklace. "Do you have your guitar with you?"

"Um," Sadie said. She reached up to clutch the pick protectively. "Yes? What are you gonna do to it?"

"We just need to invoke something into it. And carve a tiny symbol. Is that alright?"

"I guess. Like, if it helps."

Milly checked her watch and stood. "We should do it now. We have to be on the road in an hour."

Honey asked, "Where are you going?"

Milly touched the skull on her bracelet. "We have to help some friends."

————

She led them into the yard. Wisteria hung from a trellis overhead, dark and beautiful. There was a vegetable garden tucked in the back. A stretch of grass was overgrown and full of daisies except for a perfect circle cut into the middle.

Milly nodded at the circle. "Lie the guitar down in it."

Sadie did.

"Now lie down next to it."

Sadie lay on her back, feeling like an idiot. Her guitar pick necklace settled in her sharp collarbones. She kept a hand curled protectively around the handle, which was now home to a strange, thorny symbol Milly had carved with a dagger. Because she was the kind of woman who kept daggers lying around.

Sadie twisted to look up at Honey, who was standing in the long grass near her head, tugging at the wisteria. Honey mimed a kick at her.

"Keep out of the circle," Milly told her. "Now..."

She paused. Frankie had leaned over to whisper something in her ear.

Sadie looked at Honey for clarification. Honey was already staring at them, lips parting in surprise, hand clenching tighter and tighter around a clump of wisteria.

By the time Frankie leaned back, the flowers were purple pulp in her hand.

Milly nodded. "Sorry, change of plans. Get in the circle."

Sadie shuffled over to make room, dragging the guitar carefully with her.

Honey didn't move. "Why? Like, what's...why me? It's her guitar. So."

"It's her guitar," Milly agreed. "But we're going to need you two to find something to...tie it to. Something important. A place, a person, a bond."

Sadie turned her face into the grass to cool her burning cheeks.

Honey stood very still. She didn't blink. "Does it have to be something that's still...does it have to be alive?"

"No, it can be dead. It just had to matter sometime. Very, very much."

Honey swallowed. For a moment it looked like she was going to cry. Then it was gone, Honey flicking her strawberry curls out of her face as she lay down in the circle next to the guitar.

"Good," Milly told them. "Do you have something in mind?"

"No," the girls said, too loud and too fast.

"That's alright. You'll find it." Milly sunk onto her knees next to the circle. "Repeat after me: I invoke thee."

"I invoke thee," Sadie said, Honey's voice rising to

join hers. She turned to give Honey a look—what were they invoking?—but Honey's eyes were closed.

Milly said it again. Sadie felt her tongue curl around the words, still feeling like an idiot, sweat leaching from her back into the grass. What had Frankie said to Milly? Why did it make Honey react like that? *A place, a person, a bond. It doesn't have to be alive. Something that mattered.*

Sadie sucked in a breath, and reached—

—for her hand.

They're always holding hands. Swing set, classrooms, couch. They're going to be rockstars, they know it in their blood. To death and beyond, I vow to thee. Kill or die or bury a body. Forever, always, pricking their thumbs and mixing the blood, pinkie promise, jinx you owe me a soda, will you love me forever yes of course even when you get a boyfriend yes even when I get a boyfriend what a stupid question.

Once they were twin stars. Once they burned together. No matter how it ended (a raised pinkie slapped away in anger, running away and not looking back and the next day at school they didn't look at each other and days passed and then years) they still had each other, once, still would've died for each other, killed for each other, buried a body, always, I vow to thee, really truly, I do, where are you going, don't walk away, please don't walk away Sadie I don't understand just—

. . .

"—come back."

Sadie jerked up with a gasp.

Milly peered at her from the grass beyond Sadie's feet. "Hello? Are you back?"

"I'm...I'm back." Sadie wiped at her cheeks. They were wet. She tried to get her elbows up under her and slumped back to the ground, shaking.

Honey stumbled to her feet. "What the hell was *that*?"

"A blessing," Milly said. "If Sadie plays this guitar, it will stop any vampire in their tracks. Except you, of course. You're immune."

"Immune," Honey croaked. "Yay. Great. I'm gonna go."

She lurched across the yard. Before Sadie could say anything, Honey blurred into a sprint. The yard gate swung open with such force it slammed into the wall and cracked, wood chips flying.

Ivy winced. "Should we—"

"The kid's got it," Frankie said. "Kid?"

Sadie pushed herself up onto her knees. She'd felt it, for a second. That bone-deep bond they'd had as kids. She'd forgotten what it was like, *feeling* everything so much. She'd gotten glimpses this past week, but to *live* like that, heart on her sleeve, bleeding everywhere...

Sadie shuddered. She'd closed herself off so tightly, and now everything was spilling out. She felt like an open wound.

"Yikes," Frankie said. She ran into the house and

came back out with a glass of lemonade.

Sadie drank it in five huge gulps. It was sweet and cold and a little tangy, leaving a pip lodged in the back of her teeth.

"I should get her," she said, wobbling to her feet.

Milly caught her shoulder, hand dropping off it as soon as it made contact. She didn't seem like someone who was big on touching.

"Your concert is tomorrow?"

Sadie nodded numbly.

"Get him alone."

"I know." Sadie dragged a sleeve along her wet cheeks. "Good luck with...whatever you guys are doing."

Milly smiled, tight and warm. "We'll be fine. Go get your girl."

Not my girl. Sadie couldn't bring herself to say it. She nodded, forgetting to wave goodbye to the others as she ran out of the gate.

The van was empty. Sadie climbed in with a curse, throwing her guitar into the backseat. She sagged in relief when she spotted a girl at the end of the street, blurring and stopping, blurring and stopping, like Sadie trying to run during PE class.

Sadie pulled up next to her. "Don't vamp run, you're still healing!"

"Like you care," Honey snapped. She blurred again,

barely making it half a block before she stumbled to a stop, grimacing.

Sadie sped up to catch her, set the van in park, and climbed out onto the sidewalk. She reached out to touch Honey's arm. "Hon..."

"*Don't.*" Honey bared her teeth. It would've been threatening, if not for the black tears staining her cheeks. She lifted her head. Daring Sadie to say something.

Sadie averted her eyes. Her chest hurt. She'd forgotten how much it hurt to feel things this deeply.

"Y-you were an asshole too. Don't pretend like you weren't."

Honey laughed. It built and built until it turned into a scream.

"God," Sadie said, looking around at the thankfully empty street. "Be *quiet*—"

"*I* was an asshole? All I did was get new friends. I'm allowed to have more than one friend."

"You didn't just..." Sadie backed up, sucking in a breath. "You didn't just get new friends. Those girls are *mean.* And *you* were mean, you *laughed* when they made jokes about my stupid spider socks—"

"They *were* stupid!"

"I only wore them because YOU got them for me," Sadie cried. "I don't even LIKE spiders! That's all you! Remember you like spiders? Or is that all gone with your —your Kim Kardashian bullshit?"

Honey growled, stabbing a finger against Sadie's chest. "That doesn't excuse you cutting me out. You just

—one day you just…" Her face crumpled. A dark tear dripped off Honey's cheek, the liquid strange and thick, clinging to her jaw.

The words hurt. Sadie forced it up through her pinhole throat. "You were gonna leave. No, don't, I knew it. You were already pulling away, it was just a matter of time before you started ignoring me and going with those girls. That's what was always going to happen, I was just getting ahead of the curve."

"I WASN'T GONNA LEAVE," Honey screamed. There was a razor edge to her voice, metallic and inhuman, making Sadie's ears ache, her ears and her swollen throat and her stinging eyes and her heart, her stupid bleeding heart.

Honey scrubbed desperately at her black cheeks. "Sadie, holy crap! Just because your mom ditched you doesn't mean everyone is going to! You think I wanted to ignore you? I ignored you because you ignored *me*, you looked at me like I was *shit*, you were family and you dumped me like trash! I tried to make up. I tried, and you called me *shit*."

Her voice cracked. If not for the dark tears she could've been fourteen again, standing in Sadie's living room with her pinkie held out, a trembling peace offering. An olive branch. Every fight they ever had was fixed with a pinkie promise, except this one.

There was a moment. Sadie tried so hard not to remember it. But now it was fresh in her mind, that strange circle in the grass dragging them into a memory that was somehow more vivid than when they lived it, and she remembered it like she was standing on that worn carpet looking at Honey's outstretched hand.

She'd wanted to kiss her. She'd wanted it so badly: drag her in by the borrowed shirt she never got back. Bend down and kiss those pink lips she'd been staring at since before she knew why. But she was fourteen and furious, and she'd never kissed anyone before. Maybe if she had, everything would be different.

Sadie stepped forward. Seventeen and stupid, waking up her heart from a deep sleep.

Honey's lip curled. Not a snarl, but close. She stayed very still as Sadie got close, and for a second Sadie thought it would actually happen.

She touched Honey's cold cheek.

Honey growled. It broke in the middle.

"*Don't*," she hissed, and ran.

fourteen

IT WAS easy enough to find Sadie the next morning. They couldn't stay at the motel where Honey attacked a businessman in the lobby, which left them with only a few options in Lock. Honey just had to go to them until she smelled that telltale peach-salt-musk.

She stood in the motel hallway for several minutes, listening. Sadie was watching TV. Some infomercials about skin cream. When they were kids Sadie would turn on the infomercials channel and just...watch. *It's nice to think all your problems can be solved with a vacuum cleaner*, she would say.

Honey knocked.

A low curse. The scramble of footsteps. Sadie flung the door open, panting. She smelled like old sweat and liquor.

Honey flicked her hair out of her eyes, doing her best Cool, Calm, Collected (And Hotter Than You) impression. She used to practice it in the mirror.

"Hey," she said.

Sadie stared at her neck. "You're healed."

"Yup." Honey popped the *p*, dragging her shirt down to expose the shiny new skin. Other than a patch of dead white, it looked normal again.

"Where were you all night?"

Honey shrugged. "Just... walking. Anyway, we should go. I attacked a guy and his dog and he definitely called the cops."

"Oh my god. You ate the dog?"

"No." Honey scoffed. "I thought about it. Went with the guy instead. The dog bit me." She rubbed at the still-healing bite mark on her arm, annoyed.

Sadie stared at her. A strand of dark hair fell down her forehead. She was sweaty, bags under her eyes, wearing the same clothes she'd had on the day before, and she was so beautiful Honey couldn't look at her.

"What," Honey snapped. "Let's go! We have to break some speed limits if we wanna be in New Orleans by tonight."

Sadie jerked into motion. Honey leaned in the doorway and watched her haul her backpack over her shoulder and grab her suitcase and guitar.

"Got everything?"

"Uh-huh."

"Good." Honey strode off, letting the door slam with Sadie still in the room behind her.

———

It was a silent drive to New Orleans. Sadie didn't even put on a CD, so Honey was stuck trying to focus on the rumble of the highway and not Sadie's heartbeat.

The annoying thing was, it was *soothing*. If Honey could, she would've been soothed to sleep by Sadie's thumping heartbeat. Then again, that would also require her to be soothed. Honey was wound so tight a thousand-dollar massage done to whale sounds couldn't soothe her. She couldn't stop thinking about Sadie's face when she'd stepped forward to touch Honey's cheek.

She'd looked...*longing*. Like she'd been walking through the desert and Honey was a waterfall. But she didn't say sorry. Honey wanted her to say it. She wanted Sadie to *beg* for forgiveness, and Honey wasn't sure if she'd even give it.

Sadie had been her friend since grade school. Her best friend, her only friend, her confidante and partner in crime and soulmate and *whatever*, and Sadie had crapped all over it. Sure, Honey had gotten bitchy in high school. But that wasn't an excuse to treat her like crap. Honey's whole world tilted on its axis when Sadie left. She held all her new friends at arm's length until they knew she wasn't someone to talk to about real-life stuff. She didn't let herself get close to her boyfriends, even ones she actually liked. She told herself it was because they wouldn't like the real her, and some of them didn't. But there were a few who seemed like they could, laughing at the few weird insect facts she let slip and entertaining her intensity even when it stopped being cute. Not that Honey gave them much time to appreciate it. She'd break up with them when the relationship started getting too real.

Sadie had screwed her up. And she acted like it was *Honey's* fault.

They pulled into a rest stop.

Sadie paused, hand on the door handle. "I'm glad you came back."

Honey glared at her. "Because you were out of money to pay for the motel room?"

"Also that." Sadie hunched apologetically until Honey slapped a couple of twenties into her hand. "Thanks."

"Bite me." Honey flashed her teeth in a sharp smile until Sadie shut the door behind her. She flopped back against her seat, reaching to the glove box for some music. For someone who liked their CD collection so much, Sadie didn't make much use of it. It was probably the hangovers, Honey reasoned. She'd smelled it on Sadie back in the motel room. Alcohol was a worryingly familiar smell when it came to Sadie. Not that Honey cared.

She clicked open the glove box. A piece of paper sat on top of a messy CD stack.

Honey took it out. It was badly crumpled, scribbled on motel paper from a few days ago. She read the first line and froze.

Blood In A Motel Bathroom. It was scrawled up the top in hasty handwriting. The song fell together in a familiar tune as she read on:

washing up in another motel bathroom / scrub that stain right outta your mouth / we swore it was womb to tomb / but I think this is gonna go south / worst week of my life, best time I ever had / watch the teeth, baby—

The paper ripped. Honey's thumb had pierced straight through *baby*.

She threw it back in the glove box and grabbed Sadie's phone, ripping the car door open. The hinges squeaked warningly.

"Shut up," Honey told them, charging for the bathroom, almost clipping Sadie as she went. Sadie stopped.

"Where are you—"

"Gotta pee," Honey snarled.

"I thought you didn't do that anymore?"

Honey whirled on her. "It's vampire pee, GOD, Sadie, I don't tell you EVERYTHING!"

She blurred the rest of the way to the bathroom—it had access from the outside, thank god—and collapsed against the door, black tears streaming down her cheeks. She typed Sadie's passcode into her phone with trembling fingers and scrolled through her contacts until she got to H.

It rang twice. Bree Williams's voice filtered through, dry and tired.

"Are you dead?"

Honey let out a sob. "What?"

"Oh." Bree made a strained noise that meant

emotions are happening, what do I do. "You just...I was joking. Are you okay?"

Honey smeared at the black running down her cheeks. The texture was strange, thicker than normal tears. It was like wiping tar.

"Everything's really screwed up, mom."

"Okay," Bree said, with only a hint of panic. "Do you need me to come and get you?"

"No."

"Where are you? What band are you following across three states right before school starts?"

"It doesn't matter. They suck." Honey grabbed paper towels from the dispenser and started wiping. It took some serious effort to get this crap off her face, and she didn't want it to stain her clothes.

"Who are you with? I hope you're giving them gas money."

"Duh, mom." Honey sniffed. "I'm...I'm with Sadie Greer."

"Oh!" Bree's surprise was so delighted it made Honey lapsc back into tears. "How is she? I miss her."

"Yeah," Honey croaked. "I'm so...she wrote us a *song*...everything's so messed up. *I'm* so messed up. I'm so scared."

"Of what? Honey, let me come and get you. I can take time off work—"

"No." Honey wiped determinedly at her face, catching stray drips about to land on her shirt. "We gotta do one last thing. Then we're coming back. Okay?"

"Okay. If you're sure."

Honey met her own eyes in her reflection, reaching down deep inside to shadows she was only starting to discover. Her eyes filled out with liquid black, a golden circle gleaming in the center. Her teeth lengthened, sharpening into fangs. She opened her mouth, tilting it to examine the dangerous cavern.

One more night. Some mind-boggling violence. Then she could go back to hash browns and sleep.

"I'm sure," she said. Slow and careful, so she didn't slur around her fangs.

Sadie had only driven for another ten minutes before they pulled over.

Honey looked at Google Maps. They had half an hour until New Orleans.

"Did you see a raccoon?" She looked around, half-joking. "Maybe a tasty deer?"

Sadie shook her head. "You need all the strength you can get," she said, and pulled the neck of her hoodie down.

Honey's cold heart dropped into her stomach. A vein stood out in Sadie's pale skin, pulsing gently.

"I ate last night," Honey murmured.

"Yeah, but you're going toe to toe with a vampire who's way stronger than you. You need to load up. Just heal me after." Sadie pulled pointedly at her hoodie, an exclamation point against her slender neck.

Honey leaned over the gearshift cautiously. "You don't want to grab something to hit me with?"

Sadie paused. "I trust you."

Honey rolled her eyes, but Sadie just…looked at her. Head-on, like she used to. Like she *saw* her, and she wanted more.

Honey swallowed. Leaned in further until her lips skimmed Sadie's shoulder. The vein beat tantalizingly under Honey's tongue.

"I'll make it nice," she promised.

Sadie shivered. "You better."

Honey bit down. The blood flooding her mouth was almost overwhelming enough for her not to hear Sadie's pained gasp melt into pleasure as venom rushed into her system—but not quite.

Honey smiled against Sadie's neck.

fifteen

TWO CHOCOLATE BARS and a Gatorade later, Sadie was sneaking backstage in yet another bar.

"You really should be more familiar with bars," Honey told her as they walked—calmly and casually—through the DO NOT ENTER door. "Your fake ID works in towns that haven't known you since birth."

"No shit. I just drink at home, like a responsible teenager." Sadie hoisted the backpack further up her back, clutching her blessed guitar. "Okay, where's—"

"Excuse me, *who* are you?"

Sadie whirled around. A stressed woman with an earpiece and a Sharpie'd nametag that read MELISSA stood half out of a hallway door, a clipboard clutched to her chest.

"This is off limits," she continued. "The bathrooms are—"

Honey cut her off. "We're the opening act."

Sadie stared at her. Honey's smile was tight with

determination, which historically meant either they were going to get away with something or they were in big trouble. The last time Sadie saw that smile, they got free popcorn at the movies for a week. It was because they talked the manager into believing Honey was a Make-A-Wish kid, and it ended up with both of them grounded for a month, but still. Free popcorn.

Melissa frowned, looking them up and down. "You're...the Slamcocks?"

Sadie laughed shrilly.

"They're running late," Honey said smoothly. "We're Honeybloods. Last minute backups."

She slapped Sadie's guitar. Sadie batted her hand off protectively.

Honey leaned in, teeth still gritted in a smile. "You'll let a strange woman carve a creepy symbol in it, but you won't let—"

Melissa cut her off. "Everything's been cleared with Jeff?"

The girls nodded fervently.

Melissa sighed, pinching her nose. "Fine. Go get everything cleared with the soundies, they're still prepping for the Slamcocks. Watch the wires, nobody's taped them and two people have already tripped."

She fled through the door, earpiece jiggling.

Honey leaned in again, gold eyes gleaming.

"I," she whispered, "Am a *god*."

"You're a god," Sadie agreed.

Honey snickered. For a moment it was like they

weren't about to murder a guy and they hadn't had a blowout screaming match yesterday—they were just two grinning girls getting away with something stupid.

Then a guy stormed in, holding a microphone and cursing. He saw the girls and pointed.

"You. Backups. What are we setting up?"

"Uhhhh," said Honey.

Sadie lifted her guitar. "Just an amp chord. And a mic."

He clapped. "Easy. Done. Follow me."

Honey stopped him. "Before we go out, could you point us toward the little girls' room?"

They spilled into the bathroom, giggling.

"The Slamcocks really are late," Honey said as she craned her neck, sniffing for the telltale smell of rot. "I heard that lady freaking out about it while we were waiting in line."

She gave another hard sniff.

"Anything?"

"No. But nobody's in this hallway, I think we're good to—"

Sadie caught her shoulder before she could turn to the door. "Honey."

Honey's face went guarded. "Yee-es?"

The words caught in her throat. "In freshman year. I really did think you would leave."

Honey snorted bitterly. "Yeah, you handed it *great*. Now, can we—"

Sadie caught her again. Honey could push her away if she wanted, could shove her right through the wall with minimal effort. But she let Sadie stop her, let her turn her back around.

"I was jealous," Sadie admitted. "I...I wanted you to myself. I still do."

Honey blinked. Her lips parted, and anxiety and desire squirmed through Sadie's stomach in equal measures.

"Not that you can't have other people," she continued. "Obviously. But I shouldn't have...you *were* a dick. But I was, too. You're allowed to have other friends, as long as they don't, like, laugh at me and call me a loser bitch with a pathetic haircut."

"That was one time," Honey said faintly. Her hands clenched around nothing, limp at her sides. "So you still..."

"Yes," Sadie said. She laughed, the hollow noise bouncing around the empty stalls. "Obviously. I...I tried to stomp it out of me, I tried to kill everything inside me, it hurt too much. Then you turned up and you dragged me into this mess and I hated most of it and it was the best thing that ever happened to me. I've felt more alive in the last week than I have in the last three years. You, like, kind of saved me?"

She rubbed her chest. Not a demonstration—her heart hurt.

"What I'm trying to say—I mean—I'm glad you asked me to come. Hon, I—"

The door slammed open. Melissa burst in, panting.

"What are you *doing*? You're on in two minutes! Where's Jeff? He's not handling *anything* tonight."

Sadie traded another panicked look with Honey as they found themselves being frog-marched down the hallway and into the wings of a stage, where a panicked soundie was standing with an amp cord, whisper-yelling at his coworker.

Melissa dragged Sadie's backpack off and threw it in a corner, ignoring their protests.

"*Go,*" she hissed, and pushed them both.

Sadie stumbled on. Honey followed at a slow walk, the push having done nothing but confuse Melissa, who shot the girls a frown as she strode back into the wings.

Sadie held out her guitar for the soundie, then strummed obediently for the soundcheck. He gave her a thumbs-up. She returned it shakily.

"What do we do?" she whispered as Honey came up beside her. "Do we do, like, a cover? What of? What's a song we both know?"

Honey hesitated. She glanced out at the crowd, which was still thin. "Um. How about *Blood In A Motel Bathroom?*"

Sadie stared. Only when the soundie made a noise did she realize she'd almost dropped her guitar on his head.

"Sorry," she said, tugging it back up. She looked over

at Honey, who had her arms crossed, shielding her chest. "You—"

"I read it," Honey admitted. "If you want to keep something secret, find a better place than a glove box right in front of the passenger seat I'm stuck in for hours every day."

"I wasn't..." Sadie swallowed. "Do you...know it enough?"

Honey nodded.

"Are you sure? If you only read it once—"

"I know it," Honey assured her. "And every song we made up had the same tune. You even wrote a space in the middle for the screaming bit."

A light above the stage went out. Sadie jumped, but Honey just stood. It didn't make a difference, Sadie realized. She could see Sadie if the whole bar plunged into darkness.

A row of lights switched on overhead, making Sadie squint. She pressed her thumb over the symbol Milly had carved into the guitar. It was tied to their strange little childhood friendship which had gone down in flames. That was how it got its power: two girls making a blood pact on a swing. *I vow to thee.*

Honey nodded down at it. "Let's take that bad boy for a test drive. See if any assholes backstage come down with a bad case of brain bleed."

She turned to the microphone stand. Sadie took her place beside her. The overhead lights made it impossible to see anybody in the audience, which was a relief. Sadie liked performing better when she could forget anybody was watching. She hadn't played in front of anybody in years, not even her dad.

It's just Honey, she told herself, trying to make her hands stop sweating around the guitar neck. *You and Honey in your bedroom, screaming along to whatever dumb song you made up this week.*

The bar was silent. Sadie imagined how loud it must be to Honey—all those heartbeats. She watched as Honey dug in her pocket and brought out a pair of earplugs, fitting them into her ears.

"We're Honeybloods," Honey announced into the mic. "Here to rock your shit. Everybody ready?"

A few cheers went up. They were actually enthusiastic, and Sadie grinned despite the nerves warring in her gut. She always knew Honey would be good at this.

"One, two, three," Honey said.

Sadie scrabbled at her guitar. The song called for drums, but they'd never actually had a drummer. It didn't matter. Sadie strummed and Honey opened her mouth, voice rich and velvet, washing over Sadie like a balm.

"Washing up in another motel bathroom...scrub that stain right outta your mouth..."

Sadie hadn't played this tune for years. Her fingers found the chords like she'd done it yesterday, like she'd done it every day since she knew how to hold a guitar, which, for a while, was true. Some things always came back, no matter how long you left them.

Honey swayed her hips to the beat, a slow, even circle. *"We swore it was womb to tomb...but I think this is gonna go south...."*

Sadie's fingers stung. She strummed harder. The guitar pick was still around her neck. She wanted to feel this. She'd spent the last two years trying not to feel anything, she wanted to feel this, even if it hurt.

Honey's voice rose in the tiny bar. *"Worst week of my life, best time I ever had."* She turned, flashing Sadie a smile. *"Watch the teeth, babyyyy..."*

It hit Sadie like a slap, like a sugar rush, like that first shot of vodka alone in her living room. They slammed into the chorus, Sadie's heart thumping so loud they could use it for a drumbeat. Sweat pricked her scalp, her armpits, the backs of her knees. The lights bore down, turning the crowd into a white blur. And ahead of that blur was Honey: crooning, swaying, headbanging. Her hair flew around her in a strawberry blonde halo, catching the stage lights, and Sadie's breath caught so hard she fumbled the next chord.

Honey turned back again, shooting her another grin. Teasing. They were both in on the joke. They had terrible things to come, but for now they had this.

Then Honey's smile died. Her voice trailed off. She'd caught sight of something in the wings.

Sadie turned.

Deep in the wings, the singer of The Bleeding Bastards crouched in agony. His hands shook over his head. Black goo leaked out of his ears and down his cheeks. His eyes cracked open as the guitar music ebbed to a stop. He wobbled urgently to his feet.

Shit. Sadie strummed again, and the pained whine he let out was audible even from the stage.

Honey leaned back into the microphone. "Um, we have an equipment failure. Back to your regularly scheduled opening act. Slamcocks, get out here."

She grabbed Sadie's hand as they ran toward the wings, where the singer was stumbling off and a group of confused guys with guitars and frosted tips were gathered at the edge.

chapter
sixteen

THE SINGER RAN into the hall.

Honey followed, Sadie trailing behind after pausing to grab the backpack.

"Keep playing," Honey called.

Sadie strummed the chords from their song as she followed. Honey pushed the hallway doors open to find the singer collapsing to his knees, groaning. He dragged himself toward the men's bathrooms.

Honey grabbed him by the back of the neck and shoved him through the bathroom door. She leaned back to let Sadie in, still strumming, then stepped in behind her.

The door swung shut. The singer twisted onto his back, baring his teeth pathetically.

"Wait," he slurred. His bared teeth became a simpering imitation of his boyish smile. "We can work something out. You wanna be on stage? We can make it happen."

Honey planted a foot on his squirming chest. "You're a subpar indie band who tours exclusively in bars and community centers. I'll pass. Sadie?"

Sadie held out the backpack awkwardly, still strumming.

Honey fished out the ax.

The singer groaned. He turned back, going on his knees. "Wait. *Wait!*"

Honey's hands shook on the handle as she strode around to his front. His hand slipped out from under him, smashing him into the ground chin-first. He shuddered, then his whole body jerked upward—his back hit the ceiling, still shuddering.

"Wait," he repeated, dropping an inch and then floating up back to the ceiling. "I can...*we* can—"

Honey flew up to meet him, closing her hand around his throat, pressing him hard into the ceiling.

"You shouldn't have killed me," she told him. A trail of black ran down her cheek. She flipped him over with her, aiming him at the bathroom tiles.

He screamed, hands coming up to cover his head.

Honey raised the ax and slammed them into the floor. The ax came down right as he smashed into the tiles. The blade took his hands first, chopped off at the wrist. He yelled. The strumming stuttered.

"Keep going," Honey snarled at Sadie. She spat tile dust out of her mouth and raised the ax again.

Sadie resumed strumming.

"Guess you won't get to hold his rough hand while you're wasted," Honey hissed.

The singer's face twisted in pained confusion, cradling the stump where his hand used to be. "What?"

Honey swung. The next chop hit his neck. And the next. It took three in total before the singer's head lay on the tiles, spurting black blood into the cracks.

The strumming died. Honey looked over to find Sadie covering her mouth, her back against a closed stall. Black oozed toward her shoes.

Honey stepped around the growing puddles and took Sadie's face in her hands. "Hey! Hey, you're alright. It's okay. Everything's good. We fixed it."

Sadie nodded. There was a smudge of black on her cheek. Honey hadn't realized it was on her hands.

She wiped it off. "Are you going to puke?"

Sadie shook her head. "Are you..."

Honey pressed a hand over her heart. It was cold and still. How long did these things take, anyway?

Sadie frowned. "Are you...are you sure it was him?"

"Yeah. Yes, I'm...it was him. I'm..." Honey trailed off. That night was so fuzzy. They'd all bitten her, or at least they'd all been *there*. She'd had so many bite marks, and most of them were from him. It *had* to be him. Right?

The stench of rot hit her like a train. Honey turned just in time to watch the door burst open, the rest of The Bleeding Bastards rushing in and freezing when they saw their singer beheaded on the floor.

Cold fear ripped up Honey's spine.

"Well, hi," she croaked. She hefted her ax. "Who wants—"

The bassist shrieked. He charged at her in all his six-foot glory, and Honey yelped.

"PLAY, SADIE, PLAY LIKE THE—"

The bassist knocked her into the wall, tiles cracking behind them. He reared back, arm a hard line across her throat, teeth a pile of points.

He snarled, "I'm gonna—"

The rest of his sentence choked in his throat as guitar music started up. Honey shoved the arm off her neck and kicked him in the stomach. He folded like a wet paper towel. Honey lifted the ax and brought it down once, twice, three times. Black blood splattered on the mirror.

She stood, shaking. The lead guitarist was clutching his hands over his ears and dragging himself out the door. It swung shut behind him.

"So much for loyalty," Honey said. "How about—"

She stopped. The drummer wasn't on the floor. He wasn't even cringing. He was terrified, pressed back against the sinks in terror—but he wasn't bowing in agony over the guitar chords.

Honey stared at him. There, under the stink of rot and decayed blood: a heartbeat. His blood pounded. A thin line of urine tracked down his leg. He stunk like them from so much exposure, but he was human, through and through. And Honey was still a vampire. Which meant...

She looked toward the hallway the lead guitarist had crawled into.

"Huh," she said.

She stepped toward the door. She was so busy watching the door she didn't notice the knife until it was too late.

The drummer shrieked, lunging at Sadie.

"*No!*" Honey sped at him. She caught him around the middle and slammed him into the hand dryer, plastic smashing against his spine. He fell limply to the floor, unconscious.

Honey turned.

Sadie stood perfectly still. The guitar trembled in her hands. She'd held it up to protect herself.

Not high enough.

A penknife protruded from her neck. Sadie reached for it, slow and dreamlike.

"Don't," Honey blurted.

Sadie pulled it out. The drip of blood turned to a torrent, gushing out to coat her guitar pick necklace, flowing onto her ripped jeans.

"Oh," Sadie gurgled. "Crap."

She crumpled to the floor. Honey was so stupid with shock she barely managed to catch her in time, holding her up against the toilet stall.

Sadie blinked, slow and sluggish. "Never...been in the guys' bathroom before. 'S gross."

She fumbled with Honey's elbows. Another pulse of blood spurted out of her neck, catching Honey in the chin. Honey felt her tongue dart out to lick it up, automatic. Her teeth sharpened.

Sadie chuckled. The color was already draining out of her face, her already-pale skin going deathly white.

"Not dying for you," she said weakly, and laughed. She groped at the bloody mess of her neck. "Really shouldn't have said that..."

"It's not that bad," Honey told her. She pressed at the wound in Sadie's neck. Blood coursed over her fingers, hot and sticky and tantalizing. Honey leaned in like a star dragged toward a black hole and had to shake herself to stop.

"I'm...I'm gonna heal you. Hear me?"

Sadie nodded, head sagging. A tear fell down her cheek.

Honey sunk her fangs into her neck, right over the hole, pushing venom desperately into Sadie's bloodstream. Sadie's hands were so weak around her elbows, barely gripping.

Honey jerked back. Blood kept pouring. Slower, but still steady. Still too much.

"Shit," Honey said. "Okay. I'm gonna—Sadie?"

Sadie's chin dropped to her chest. Her eyelids fluttered. The wound was too deep, Honey realized. She'd bleed out before the veins closed up.

She let out a sob. It echoed around the ruined bathroom.

"Sadie?" She shook her. Sadie's head lolled around and came to a rest on top of Honey's cold hand.

"Shit," Honey said again. "Oh god, oh *shit*. Don't make me lose you. We just got each other back."

Sadie didn't respond. Something rattled in her chest. She was inhaling the blood. Her heart beat slower and slower.

Honey didn't think. She reached over to the penknife lying next to them and slashed her own palm open. She held it up to Sadie's slack mouth, pushing until black blood leaked past her lips.

"Come on," she whispered. "Please."

She pressed until Sadie's chin was smeared with black. Then she cut her tongue on her teeth. She took Sadie's white face in her hands and kissed her, some childhood instinct bleeding through. Sleeping Beauty, Snow White. They used to act out the stories, rock-paper-scissoring who got to play the prince. Honey kissed her harder, willing whatever messed up magic they had between them to work once more. A symbol carved into a guitar, pinkie promises, pricking their fingers on a swing. They'd been mixing their blood since they were children, what was one more time?

She was still kissing Sadie when Sadie's heart stuttered to a stop.

chapter
seventeen

SADIE GREER WOKE UP DEAD.

Black stained her chin. Her mouth tasted like blood, bitter and beautiful.

"Hon," she croaked.

Honey's face shot into view above her, golden-black eyes lighting up in a blazing, gap-toothed smile.

"Hi! Holy crap, you're back. That was wild. You ate the crap out of the drummer."

Sadie smacked her lips, chasing the delicious taste. "I what?"

Honey eased Sadie onto her knees. The bathroom was even more wrecked than when Sadie passed out—the ceiling was cracked, the beheaded singer and bassist piled bloody and terrible up against the door, and now another body joined them. The drummer stared up at the dented ceiling with blank eyes, his face a mask of horror. His throat had been ripped out.

"Oh," Sadie rasped. "Crap."

Honey wiped her face with a paper towel. Sadie tilted her head back, letting her clean her chin, her brows, pinching paper around her septum piercing. She was too groggy to do anything else.

"The cops are on their way," Honey said as she blotted blood from Sadie's cheeks. "Probably with a SWAT team. I barricaded us in. Want to escape out the window?"

Sadie turned to look blearily at the window. It wasn't big enough for Honey's hips, but they could change that with brute vampire strength.

"Cool," she slurred. She reached up to still Honey's hand.

Honey was beautiful. This was true before, but it was even more true with Sadie's new vampire vision. Her skin shone under the mess. Her curls were stiff with blood. Black streaked her cheeks. Not blood— tears. She'd been crying. Sadie had never seen anyone look so relieved as Honey cupping Sadie's cheeks, looking at her like she'd stolen her back from death. She *had* stolen her back, feeding life back into her mouth. What right did death have over Sadie, when Honey was right here?

Sadie swallowed. "We need to stop having romantic moments in bathrooms."

Honey giggled wetly. "But it's our brand! We can't stop now." She tilted her head. "Okay. *That's* a siren."

Sadie closed her eyes. There, beyond the panicked whispers in the emptied-out bar and the general buzz of traffic—a siren. A few of them, actually. Screaming right toward them, maybe a block away.

Sadie wobbled up, grabbing her guitar. Honey eased an arm around her shoulder to make sure she didn't fall, and flew them up to the window.

Sadie landed in a dumpster. The back parking lot was empty. It must've really cleared out after all that screaming.

Honey landed behind Sadie in the dumpster with a neat thump, shooting her a nervous smile. The parking lot had been full when they got here. Steve-van was two blocks away in an alley.

"I'm still kinda weak," Sadie told her. "Can you, like…pick me up and run so fast nobody can see us?"

Honey grinned. She leaned in until their noses brushed, and her black-streaked freckles looked like the rest of Sadie's un-life. She scooped Sadie up into a piggyback.

"Better hold on tight, spidermonkey," she whispered.

12 hours later, the news stations were still quiet.

"The band wasn't big," Honey said from behind her, legs crossed on the motel bed. "They didn't even have socials; it was ridiculous."

Sadie lay her head on Honey's lap, watching *Gilmore Girls* play from the phone they'd propped up on the pillows. "Probably for the best, if they were killing people in every town they toured in."

She paused Rory and Lorelai's rapid-fire dialogue and scrolled through the local news for New Orleans. Still no articles about two band members found beheaded and one drained of blood in a bar bathroom right before their show.

"Weird," Honey whispered. "Has Milly replied?"

Sadie checked her notifications. "Not yet."

"Maybe she's dead." Honey twisted a strand of Sadie's damp hair around her finger and tugged. "Seems like she dealt with a lot of dangerous magic shit."

Sadie batted her hand away. "She better not be dead. I have no clue how to track down your sire. And we don't have anyone else to ask about other ways to turn me back."

She turned her phone off. The room plunged into darkness. It didn't matter. They could see each other perfectly.

Honey leaned back against the headboard. "It kinda sounded like there weren't."

"There have to be." Sadie pushed herself up until she was looming over Honey. "I'm not killing you. I'd rather be a vampire forever."

Honey stared up at her. Save for the ceiling fan, the room was silent. *Not even breathing*, Sadie thought. *Not even heartbeats.* Her heart lay still and cold inside her chest, but she'd never felt so alive than right now, lying on a cheap motel bed with the childhood friend she'd scorned for so many years.

If Sadie could blush, she would. She leaned against Honey, cheek pillowed on her shoulder.

"I need to call my mom," Honey said. "We're going back home, right?"

"We have to leave today. School starts soon."

Honey twisted, her chin brushing Sadie's head. "So you're coming back for senior year?"

"Sure," Sadie said. "Not like I got anything else on."

"Hmm. Gonna be a weird year."

"It's gonna be a weird *life*," Sadie corrected. "Un-life. Whatever."

It *would* be weird. And scary. And messy. The idea of never drinking booze again made Sadie squirm. She had no idea how they were going to get blood in their hometown. They had animals in the woods, but would it be enough to keep them fed? Could they be around humans all day, or would it get too much? What kind of life were they heading into?

I don't care, as long as I get to spend it next to you. The words lurked dangerously behind her teeth. It was too much. She couldn't say it. She settled for curling harder into Honey's unrelenting side and closing her eyes.

Not sleeping. Never sleeping again. Just existing next to each other in comfortable silence until it was time to go.

End.

more honey and blood
to come

Want to find out what happens next in the **HONEYBLOODS** series? You can order the next book at my website.

thank you

Thank you so much for reading HONEYBLOODS!

If you want to support me, please leave a review on Goodreads, Amazon and any social media of your choice. You can get updates on my upcoming books (and a free spooky sapphic novella) by subscribing to my newsletter! Sign up by visiting my website at isbelleauthor.com.

You can find me on Tiktok @i.s.belle_writes and on Instagram @isbelleauthor.

acknowledgments

Let's thank my nemesis first! Chloe Spencer (fellow author of sapphic horror romances and the best nemesis a gal could ask for) was a beta reader AND my American consultant on this project. Thank you Chloe for your awesome beta feedback, and for entertaining all the confused Instagram messages from a bewildered kiwi.

Any American reading this - learn to read a road map, guys. Google Maps can't save you all the time. One day your phone WILL die when you're in the middle of nowhere, and not all cars have GPS. Also, get better coffee. I love you.

Thank you to my cover artist Sophie Zuckerman (@dextrose.png on Insta!) for the baller cover. Still swooning over all the little details. 'Twas great working with you, can't wait to see what you do with the rest of the covers for the HONEYBLOODS series.

Thank you to my wonderful formatter, Edward Giordano, and Catriona Turner, my editor. You two are an absolute pleasure to work with, and I'm always blown away by the results. A great big forehead kiss for the both of you.

about the author

I. S. Belle is a Young Adult author who lives in New Zealand. She has a Creative Writing Masters from the International Institute of Modern Letters. She works in a bookstore and stops to pat dogs in the street. If you have a dog and your local bookshop allows pets - for the love of booksellers, please bring them in.

also by i. s. belle

BABYLOVE SERIES

BABYLOVE

SUGARSNAP

SWEETHEARTS

ZOMBABE

ZOMBABE

HONEYBLOODS SERIES

HONEYBLOODS

GIRLS NIGHT

GIRLS NIGHT - Coming April 2024

www.ingramcontent.com/pod-product-compliance
Lightning Source LLC
Chambersburg PA
CBHW050143110726
47898CB00008B/2651